The Reviled

THE REVILED

Dark Fey Book I

Cynthia A. Morgan

Copyright (C) 2014 Cynthia A. Morgan
Layout design and Copyright (C) 2020 by Next Chapter
Published 2020 by Shadow City – A Next Chapter Imprint
Cover art by Cover Mint
This book is a work of fiction. Names, characters, places, and incidents are the product of the author's imagination or are used fictitiously. Any resemblance to actual events, locales, or persons, living or dead, is purely coincidental.
All rights reserved. No part of this book may be reproduced or transmitted in any form or by any means, electronic or mechanical, including photocopying, recording, or by any information storage and retrieval system, without the author's permission.

*Dedicated to my Loving Family and Friends
Who have supported me
For many years.*

And

*Special Thanks to Jena Wolgemuth
For her tireless enthusiasm and motivational encouragement.*

I am truly Blessed.

An Introduction

Welcome to mythical, enchanted forest of Jyndari and the Village of Hwyndarin where The Fey of the Light, who are Light loving Fey, reside.

Where there is Light there is also darkness and the Fey of the Light live in careful vigilance, protecting themselves from the Dark Fey who are known by many names, such as the Fallen, the Dark Ones, and most particularly The Reviled. They live in a realm of darkness and shadow known as the Uunglarda.

Although their two realms exist in close proximity, most Fey of the Light have never seen an actual Dark Fey and many Dark Fey only encounter very young Fey of the Light, yet crossings and abductions happen every day.

As their temples are desecrated, homes are pillaged and plundered, and the peaceful tranquility so important to the Fey of the Light is repeatedly shattered, the Fey Guard stand as protectors. They are mighty in battle and fierce in their vigilance to protect the fragile balance of life for the peaceful Fey of Light.

All Fey are born with special abilities, or gifts, such as telepathy, empathy, discernment, or the ability to dream walk. Many also have a gift of magic, though not all, such as spell-casting, enchantment, light bending or element wielding. While the Fey of the Light are beautiful and live harmoniously, the Reviled Fey are the opposite. They revere darkness and fill their lives with cruelty and violence, but all Reviled Fey begin their lives as Fey of the Light. The change comes only if they are abducted as childfey and forced to undergo the Integration, a process of intentional neglect and cruelty designed to twist them away from the Light.

This level of horror is not incorporated into the Dark Fey Trilogy simply for the sake of it. One does not need to open the pages of a book to discover the unthinkable, as the darkness typically embodied in fantasy genre stories by some terrifying being or creature is very much alive in our own reality and this is the underlying motivation for the darkness woven into Dark Fey. It is based in great part on the terrifying, yet true-life events of the Lord's Resistance Army or LRA, a rebel militant group in Uganda that has for over 20 years abducted children from their homes; forcing them to commit horrifying acts of violence against each other and their own people. These children and other child soldiers like them suffer a very real Integration and, like the childfey of Jyndari, they endure violence and cruelty at the hands of truly sadistic overlords. This is how the Reviled came to life and became the horrifyingly cruel beings depicted in Dark Fey.

This story shares the Power of Hope, Acceptance and Forgiveness through the ideal that you can change the world, if you take Positive Action to Create Change by doing what is Right.

Many times during your journey through the Dark Fey Trilogy, you will encounter words that seem to be capitalized for no apparent reason; yet, it should be noted, these capitalizations are anything but random. They mark either proper nouns, such as Fey of the Light, the Temple, Fey Guards, the Reviled, or the Light, which is not simply a glimmering of illumination, but a connotation that is highly important in the spirituality of Fey. If a word holds specific meaning, it may also be capitalized, such as See, Know, or Understand. You may encounter such words when they are in reference to a Fey gift, such as telepathy, empathy, or discernment, and they carry significant weight so, in order to emphasize their importance, capitalization is used.

Join me as we embark into this realm of Light and Dark. Allow your imagination take over as you experience the Jyndari forest and the Fey of the Light's struggle with the Reviled. Let the Light reach outward from these pages and draw you into on a journey that promises not only to enchant, but to change your way of thinking.

Preface

The only way to achieve Peace is to become Peace.

Not a day had gone by during Ayla's childhood years when she had not been told the tales of The Reviled, tales which were meant to frighten her into absolute vigilance to always be wary of the darkness where the Reviled could lie in wait. She learned how they came in the hours of the night to steal away the innocent or to ruin the pure. Takers of the Innocent, Child Wraiths, Corruptors of the Beloved, Dark Ones; the Reviled had many names and she knew them all because she was different, set apart from other Fey by her innate abilities, which were given, it was said, by the Wisest of the Wise. She would be a light for her people, a Guardian of Cherubs. Her course was set from her earliest years.

It had not taken long for her parents and attendants to determine that she had remarkable talents unlike those of other Fey children. She could distinguish truth from lies as a falcon sees its prey in the long grasses. She could look into the eyes and see the soul, discerning beyond all the complications of guise. Empathy ran so deep within her that she could, under circumstances of extreme duress, take on the pain of another and ease their suffering. These gifts first drew attention to her, but they also set her apart and isolated her from the others.

Even from her nursery years, the tears or hurts of any of her playmates would draw her to them like a moth to flame. She would sit quietly by and their crying would subside or she would hold their hand and their pains would diminish. These first indications of her extraordinary capabilities brought her under the scrutiny of many, but ultimately led her toward the Temple.

AylaYna, the only daughter of AyannaDvnna and Bryndan, grew up in the village of Hwyndarin, an artisan's sanctuary set deep in the primordial forests of Jyndari, Land of the Fey. Here the breathtaking handcrafts of hundreds of Jyndari's finest artisans accompanied her throughout her childing years. As a childfey she was guided by scholars who filled her mind with images of good and evil, black and white, Darkness and Light; there were no gray areas, no middle grounds. She knew only truth. While her friends sat in cheery classrooms and learned the skills that would set their lives into balance and equanimity, she learned about the secret arts, about incantations and magic, which were hidden from all but a privileged few.

She learned how to battle evil with the words of the Ancients using intonations in her own language, the Common Tongue, as well as in Dlalth, the desecrated language of the Reviled. She practiced her growing skills in daily sessions that would leave her both mentally and physically exhausted, but her ability with incantations could not be left to chance. They were a matter of life or death. Day after long day, she honed her skill with artful words, as well as her talents of healing through empathy, by visiting the sick and the aged and she discovered that the use of these healing gifts would drain her own energy by an equal proportion to that which she used to ease or cure. As a result, she needed to also learn how to protect herself from her own empathic inclinations; how to use this particular gift with deliberate caution so she would not endanger herself. She also studied the mystical practices of Seeing.

Her closest friend, Nayina, learned to sew fine silks and embroider with gossamer threads that mimicked sunlight. She was taught to play the flute and the magical Fey instrument of mind and emotion called the Hudarin. She learned to weave the magic of grace and serenity into the embodiment of happiness, which would give her life purpose and stability, but AylaYna was sent off on daily treks to the Temple to learn about the banished and the lost. She was taught no other trade or skills and she lived each day with the shadow of fear.

As a youth, images of Dark Fey, those who were lost by the consequences of their own foul deeds, haunted her dreams. She slept little during these frightening years and read often. She read the ancient texts about the Fallen who could not love, could not create joy or light or bring peace and harmony, could not admire beauty or talent without avarice, could not feel compassion for another and could not bring life into the world in the form of innocence. She learned that the Dark Fey could not reproduce, so they would come in the shadows to steal away unattended childfey, taking them back to their dark realm. Those childfey, once taken, were condemned and lost as surely as their abductors.

The Dark Ones lived in the realm of eternal darkness, The Uunglarda, and could only enter into the realm of Light, into Jyndari, through portals that existed in the unlighted shadows of nightfall. They had many portals of entrance. Any deep shadow could conceal a Dark One and the Fey of the Light were vigilant in setting lamps, torches and candles so no corner stood in obscurity. Mirrors in darkness, unlighted wells, the dying embers of a fire that stood unguarded or the very rare faerie ring that no longer flowered gave the Fallen a place to cross. They came in darkness, they brought darkness with them, and they were the epitome of everything that was not light, bright, and beautiful.

During Ayla's middling years, those years between innocent childhood and responsible adulthood, she was given a tenuous measure of freedom. With the majority of her education completed, she was required to attend her lessons in the Temple less frequently and could embark upon those more immediate concerns of laughter, flirtation and youthful love. She was given the happy task of guarding the village's childfey during their play hours and was even called upon during special occasions to watch over the young ones of different families while the adults were away. It was her gifts which set her apart and which led her to become a Guardian, it was her education and knowledge of the Dark Fey that empowered her to take up such an important task at so young an age, and it was her own joy in being with the beautifully innocent and uncomplicated that made her not mind such a loss to her own social affairs.

Chapter One

The afternoon was warm and full of birdsong. The childfey she guarded were playing contentedly in the gamesyard and Ayla, along with her friend Nayina, was resting in the shade of a broad archway of flowering wisteria. The bordering forest encircling the gamesyard on all but one side was quiet on that unusually warm day, as if all its myriad inhabitants lay resting during the heat of the day. Its dark canopy spread invitingly cool, green shadows upon the ground at its feet, enticing even the most wary to step into its shadowed depths. Ayla and her friend sipped refreshing mint tea, fanned themselves absently with their translucent wings, and spoke of unimportant matters. The day was calm and quiet, filled with giggles and warmth, yet, unexpectedly, a fleeting shadow caught Ayla's glimmering amber eyes.

Turning her head sharply in the direction of the forest, she could not disguise her distraction as she sought the elusive image at the border of the woodland. Nayina paused as well and turned to watch her friend with curiosity, fully aware of her gift of sight and the fact that she saw far more than the average Fey. When she looked, Nayina could see nothing except green shadow and shaggy undergrowth, but Ayla's eyes were fixed on something and her mouth fell open in a gape.

"What do you see Ay?" Nayina inquired softly. Her friend shook herself and turned back to face her with a shrug and a smirk.

"Nothing, I guess," she replied offhandedly, taking her glass in hand once more and bringing the cool beverage to her lips. "A shadow, a flutter, probably nothing more than a deer," she offered more obligingly as she turned back to look once again upon the playing younglings. Nayina accepted this explanation of her odd behavior, but she did not fail to notice her friend's repeatedly furtive glances toward the same direction of woodland where she had previously gazed so intently and she did not fail to see the puzzlement in her expressive amber eyes.

She said nothing more about it, but Ayla found it difficult to keep her thoughts on those whom she guarded. As the afternoon waned and parents came to collect their wee cherubs, Ayla and her friend bid each other good eventide and went toward their separate homes. Yet even as she traversed the sparkling alley of cedars, which led from the daylight nursery where she spent much of her time, and the diminutive cottage she called home on the borders of the village, she saw and heard little. Her thoughts were turned inward as she mulled over what she had seen or, at least, what she thought she had seen.

A Dark One.

Shaking her head, she scoffed aloud. It could not have been. The Dark Ones could not enter the realm of Jyndari during daylight, it was impossible, despite the fact that what she had seen had been immersed in the green shadows of the forest and protected from the rays of the sun by the duskiness of the woods. She had never heard of a Dark One being seen during the day tide, so it certainly could not have been one of the Reviled. She argued with her own thoughts, turning the possibilities over and over in her mind, shifting her opinion first in one direction and then another.

What she had seen, what she thought she saw, had been everything she ever imagined a Dark One to be: dreadful in appearance, menacing in action, demon-like, drawing shadows unto itself like smoke filling a room, but she had only seen a fleeting shadow. For one brief moment it lingered in the darkness of the undergrowth like a wolf, slinking secretly along its way. It could have been anything. Shuddering involuntarily, she shook her head again. Certainly it had been a wolf or a deer. Surely her fearful mind, filled with years of dark imagery and whispers of dread, had seen only the fleeting shadow of an animal in the dim light beneath the trees and had invented the remainder.

She spent her eventide alone, making certain to light candles in every room and out in her small garden, as well. She sat in silence and studied the writings contained within an aged, little book: the Dark Texts, wherein were contained the collected warnings about, signs of, and protections from the Reviled. Many times during her solitary read, her head snapped up at an unexpected sound or suspected movement, but each time it was only her fear that haunted her.

At last, soothed by her research and her repeated self-assurances of her own silliness, she went to bed.

The balm of early summer advanced and Ayla kept her regular schedule of morning practices and learning at the Temple, luncheons with her closest and, in truth, her only friend, Nayina, and afternoons filled by the giggles and coos of her precious, entrusted ones. After those responsibilities were discharged, she would often attempt to join in the revelry of other youthful Fey who were closest to her in age, joining small gatherings or buoyant parties during the coolth of eventide, but very often she would return home afterward disappointed by her own inabilities to connect with or even understand the complexities of youthful jocularity and flirtation. Ever more often she felt doomed to a life alone with her fears and suspicions.

* * *

"I promise, you will like him," Nayina coaxed her one steamy afternoon in the variable shade of their now green and flowerless Wisteria arch near the gamesyard. "He is just your age and he is quiet, like you."

Ayla listened to her friend's optimistic enticements, but grimaced. "Perfect. We shall spend the evening staring at our feet in utter silence."

Her friend sighed impatiently at her cynical remark, but Ayla conceded. "I shall go. I must make a greater effort, I am completely aware of it. Besides, I have never actually been to Summerfest before. Must I dress in anything special or bring anything?"

Nayina could scarce contain her excitement. It was not very often her sheltered friend agreed to join in during celebration time, especially if it also meant entertaining the attentions of someone of the opposite sex. "It is not a masque, just a party; an excuse to go out under the twilight, dance and make merry. If you want to bring something, bring some of your honey mead you are always drinking in private. It is made for sharing, after all."

Ayla leaned closer and drew a secretive, diaphanous wing around them. "What is he like?" she queried with open interest. She had precious little experience with malefey. Few found her odd upbringing appealing and even fewer found her quiet, reserved nature tempting. Nayina smiled, because, although Ayla was a beautiful young Fey, she had never had a proper suitor and she felt this was unfair and unjustified. Ayla was extremely intelligent and interesting to talk to and she was as inclined to mirth and joviality as any youth. One simply had to gain her trust.

"Oh, he is so very nice, Ay, not conceited or arrogant in any way. He is a book-learner, like you. His parents sent him off to the Temple to study the Ceremonies of the Shifting Seasons and the Rites of Entrance and such as that. They dedicated him to be a Celebrant."

Ayla listened intently, her thoughts fascinated by the possibilities this young Fey presented. Perhaps he would be the one to finally understand her. "And is he fair?" she whispered coyly, receiving in answer a fervent nod of approval from her eager friend.

"He is *so* fair! Blonde hair so bright it is nearly platinum, eyes so blue they are said to be the rarest shade of cerulean, and his wings! Oh Ay, you will simply melt when you see him!" They giggled in secretive delight and unfurled their wings to let in the trace of afternoon breeze. The remainder of the day was spent in frivolous chatter and Ayla was truly happy as she fluttered home to prepare for what promised to be her first pleasantly memorable gathering.

The vale selected for Summerfest was on the boundary of the village, set against the backdrop of Veryn Falls, a waterfall that plummeted from the peaks of the Ryvyn Mountains. Splashing from the heights hundreds of feet above, Veryn Falls' crystalline waters were cushioned by a multitude of moss-covered bastions and ivy-laden arches before it fell into an emeraldine pool at its base that stretched out its bountiful hand and flowed through the village, supplying water and life to all. The broad clearing around its precincts sparkled with hundreds of tiny lanterns strung through the surrounding forest canopy and was brightened by cheerful fires and glowing torches scattered throughout. Tables of food and vessels of drink were placed advantageously, musicians played the flute and the drum, lacewings flitted and darted, and the entire area was alive with palpable joy and anticipation.

Ayla and Nayina arrived somewhat later than expected, for even as excited as she was Ayla needed quite a few last minute reassurances before she agreed to set off with her friend. As they crossed the glowing alleys of cedars and beech, they talked about the young malefey they would meet that evening and the promise of flirtations they would have. Although their discourse was light, Ayla's thoughts were troubled. She was aware of a presence pursuing them. It kept to the shadows deep in the forest and she perceived it more with her mind than her eyes, yet it was undeniably present. She said nothing to her friend, half convinced that it was her own nervousness that set her on edge and made her fear the darkness around them, but when they arrived, distracted by her unsettling musings, Ayla hovered shyly behind her amiable friend and listened, without joining in, to her vivacious banter.

"Ay, this is Mardan. Mardan, may I introduce my best friend, AylaYna."

She had fallen into her own thoughts and had not been aware of his approach or of Nayina's polite conversation with him, but suddenly and without fore notice Ayla found herself confronted by the most handsome young Fey she had ever seen. His blond hair, cropped unusually short and full of curls, was nearly white in the sparkling light around them and his eyes were indeed the most breathtaking sky-blue imaginable, stealing her breath away as well as her voice. She bowed awkwardly to him as he smiled and inclined to her, but she could think of nothing to say.

"She is a bit shy, but if you are patient, you will not be disappointed." Nayina leaned nearer to him and spoke softly in Mardan's delightfully pointed ear. He smiled graciously and reached for Ayla's hand.

"I hate parties. Shall we go sit by the falls and watch the lacewings?" he suggested with conspicuous courtesy and, without waiting for her to either agree or disagree, led her off in the direction of Veryn Falls. Ayla glanced back at her friend with a raised brow of surprise and a delighted smile and Nayina turned away with a giggle of glee, hoping for the best.

Mardan's hand was warm over her own and did not tremble as hers did with distinct nervousness. He said nothing as they swept over the party towards the softly 'plashing waters of the falls and she stole the moment to inspect him with an inquisitive gaze. He wore festive clothes; a silken shirt of silvery-violet and leather pants of deep emerald green, the vivid colors accentuating the whiteness of his magnificent, white, feathered wings. Of course she knew all malefey had such powerful wings, sometimes twice as long as they were tall, but even with such knowledge she could not take her eyes from him; he was tall and strong of stature and simply breathtaking in his male beauty.

They alighted on the cool, damp moss surrounding the falls and she smiled at the refreshing touch of the viridian waters trapped within the plush carpet of green beneath her feet. Mardan looked down upon her and smiled as well, patiently waiting for her to breach the silence. She stammered uncertainly, then shook her head.

"I am sorry; I am simply not very good at conversation," she apologized with a self-deprecating sigh, expecting him to make a concurring, derogatory remark, but he only shook his head and continued to stare down at her with an amiable grin.

"Neither am I really." He had been told by Nayina that she was as funny and light-spirited as any other Fey, but her upbringing by gloomy theologians had made her almost unbearably cautious. He understood this aspect of the scholar's impact on a young person, having experienced it firsthand himself, and was determined to draw her out in spite of her uncertainties.

Watching the reflected light of the falls dance over her coppery tresses and glimmer in her amber eyes, he tried not to notice her painfully inept flirting ability. She was lovely; there could be no denying the fact, and he did not mind her reserved nature, as it was far more agreeable than the overzealous bubblings and blatherings of some. Slender and delicately graced, her ivory complexion hinted at the color of the palest rose; her lacy, gossamer wings were alluringly elegant and her mannerisms were demure and poised.

"Great, we can sit in silence and stare at our feet," she murmured in a rueful jest, anticipating that at any moment he would excuse himself from her disagreeable company, but her sarcasm made him laugh and the sound melted her heart. She glanced up at him in surprise and then smiled dimly.

"I would have no qualms about staring at your feet," he hinted cautiously, seeking any measure of reassurance that she was pleased by his attention and he was not disappointed. She grasped his hand more securely and turned a coy shoulder to him, her wings fluttering in her delight and this simple indication of her contentment was all he needed.

They walked for a long while around the emeraldine pool at the base of the falls and then sat on a nearby bench of marble and rose-quartz stone, watching the lacewings dart and flutter in the sparkling light. He spoke softly to her of his training at the Temple and his parent's hopes that he would become a Celebrant, a high priest of ceremonies. She shared her own unusual upbringing. She made little mention of her uniquely special abilities, but explained her specific training in relation to the Dark Ones in preparation of her life as a Guardian.

They spoke softly; they sat closely, and they shared the eventide quietly as the revelry went on without them. His touch became lighter, more captivating, and her smiles grew more blushing and breathless. The eventide's breezes were cooler than was comfortable so near to the falls, but they were reluctant to leave such pleasing surroundings so he sheltered her from the chill with his broad, arched wings attentively. Several times, when silence fell between them, he gazed down upon her ardently and had to force himself back into conversation.

In what seemed like moments the midnight horns called to all, announcing the end of the day and the beginning of night and she knew, as the lights faded, safety indoors was essential. Could it be possible they had spent hours in each other's company rather than minutes? She gazed up at him and sighed.

"We must go," she said with evident disappointment in her voice. It was the last thing in the world she wished to do. Mardan stood and took her by both hands, returning her gaze with a warm smile.

"I shall not dispute that which you know so well; I shall only point out that such a pronouncement makes me exceedingly sad," he said in a heavy tone and she closed her eyes, awash in emotions utterly unfamiliar to her.

"You are so poetic," she sighed under her breath, almost unaware of the fact that she had actually spoken the words aloud and he smiled even more affectionately at her.

"May I have the honor of escorting you to your door?" he asked quietly and she nodded without a sound. They left the party together and crossed the alleyways with deliberate slowness, loathe to part from each other. When they reached her small cottage he circled above with her, unwilling for their evening to end in spite of the fact that everywhere lanterns were burning low and fires were being extinguished. He glanced down upon her unassuming cote and private little garden lined with herbs and edible flowers, filled with birdhouses and lanterns that were a picture of simplicity and the smile that had turned the corners of his handsome mouth all evening grew broader.

They alighted by the front door at last and he turned to capture her in his encircling wings before she could step back. He drew her hands, which he had scarcely released all evening, closer to his broad chest, nearer to his heart so she might feel it pounding, and gazed down upon her with all the warmth he felt glimmering in his brilliant eyes. She gasped at his close embrace and telling stare. She was foreign to love, but she did not pull away from him.

"I have a confession to make, Ayla."

She gazed up at him curiously.

"I had a far more pleasant evening tonight than I anticipated." His honesty brought a smile and a blush to her face.

"As did I, Mardan; I was so afraid…" her voice trailed off as he raised her hands to his lips and kissed her fingers softly. Her head spun with dizzying sensations at the warm touch of his mouth, her lashes fluttered and her vigilance faltered. Drawing her closer with his hands as well as his embracing wings, he leaned nearer to kiss her gently upon her lips. She froze at the unfamiliar contact, then melted.

His kiss lingered, tantalizing her for long, breathless moments, but it id not deepen. He kissed her lips, then traced the delicate contours of her cheeks and nose, teasing the sensitive pulse rushing at her temples, tempting her to lean back into his arms so he could whisper soft kisses over the arch of her neck. She shuddered with pleasure and a sigh rushed from her lips. Pausing, he drew back and breathed deeply, smiling at her after a moment of profound concentration to regain control over his own hammering senses. They stared at each other.

"I should like to see you again, AylaYna, very much so," he said in a heavy tone and she beamed at him, overjoyed.

Chapter Two

As the beaming light of a new day glimmered over the distant horizon, Ayla lay in her bed awake and starting at the ceiling as her thoughts replayed, over and again, every moment she had spent with Mardan. Nothing could compare to the joy she felt at that moment or the anticipation she suffered as she counted each minute until she could see him again. Although they had only parted hours before and he would be leaving Hwyndarin to return to his studies at the Temple, she knew she would see him again. She absolutely knew it and that knowledge was sufficient to see her through. At last, she closed her eyes and sighed with heavenly contentment.

Birdsong filled the air outside her open window as the light of morning stole closer through the emerald shadows of the forest and there was no immediate indication that she was not on her own. As she lay, curled beneath her bedcovers trying to capture a few moments of precious sleep, she became aware of a sensation she could neither name nor recognize. It was not fear she felt, yet her eyes snapped open at the discovery and she gazed around the dim room, repeatedly reassuring herself that all was well and that her night lantern was still aglow.

She could neither see nor hear anything amiss, yet her acute senses warned her of an indistinct presence. Stretching out her sensitivity like a panther scenting the air for prey, she failed to discover the precise reason for her uneasiness, but could not assure herself that there was no reason for it either. She searched the corners for shadows, but there were none. She raised herself up in her bed and peered out the open window into the garden, hoping to see the rosy glow of sunlight illuminating all, cascading through the dark green canopy, but shadows haunted the woods just beyond her garden gate.

Ayla stole to the window and gazed out, sensing the presence. There was no shred of doubt in her mind, but she could see no one, either in her bedchamber, in the garden outside or the woods beyond. Nevertheless, she stretched her senses a bit farther, ignoring the ever present warnings that swirled in her mind when she relied solely upon her empathic ability. It was equally advantageous and dangerous to use her senses to read another. She could often know a person's intentions far sooner than when she relied upon her five senses alone; however, one could never be certain of the emotional or mental stability of the one being read. She could easily become overwhelmed by powerful emotion, lose her thoughts as well as her self-control, and become entangled in the intensity surrounding her mind.

With a sudden stab of recognition, she realized that *he* was there. Although she had no physical proof that the presence she sensed was either male or female, she inscrutably knew it to be male. It was the same presence she had been aware of in the gamesyard of the nursery, the same one she had sensed before Summerfest. A lingering, stealthy shadow in the corner of her gaze made her turn her head sharply towards the dimly lit woodland, but she could see no one and after a moment longer the feeling disappeared.

He had gone.

* * *

"Who is he?" Nayina asked when Ayla related her experience a few days later during one of their luncheons. Ayla shrugged uncomfortably. There was always the possibility that she could be utterly wrong about her assumptions.

"I do not know. Maybe it is someone who likes me, but is even more shy than I." She laughed at the thought and shook her head. "Or it may not be a person at all."

"Just your imagination? I do not think so." Nayina interjected with obvious skepticism.

"I could simply be misinterpreting what I am sensing. That is the trouble with 'reading', you can misunderstand what you think you are sensing. It could be nothing more than a self-aware animal, of which there are many, and I could be seeing it as something else."

Nayina stared at her long-time friend with uncertainty, torn between impatience with her ambiguity and the natural inclination to be concerned about such an odd occurrence. Ayla often let her clairvoyant abilities run away with her, resulting in hurt feelings and humiliations, but if she was, indeed, sensing a person she had every reason to be wary. She suggested that a conversation with the Elders might help set her mind at ease, but Ayla shook her head fervently.

"I will not bring them into it, not yet anyway. You know as well as I do they would have the entire village in chaos before nightfall with secret investigations, questionings and Seeings. No, I will be sure of things myself before I do anything." She knew she was looked upon with disparagement already and she did not, under any circumstance, wish to fuel the fire with wild reports of unseen phantoms haunting her garden. In such an event, the Elders could easily call her back to the Temple permanently, supposing her unstable in everyday life. She simply could not bear such a thought.

Nayina altered their conversation to a lighter theme and spoke about Mardan and her friend's feelings for him, as Ayla could be convinced to talk about him for hours with very little enticement. They spent the afternoon at the gamesyard watching over the little ones of the village and singing the praises of young, handsome malefey and not a trace of uneasiness crept into Ayla's mind to disrupt the pleasantness of their day.

Returning to her quiet cottage before sundown, she carefully lit all the evening lamps, prepared a small meal and then sat reading in her garden until the darkness of nighttide urged her indoors. Secured against intrusion by the steady glimmer of light filling her home, she decided to retire early. She was inexplicably curious to discover if the presence would return, if she would recognize it as the same male entity and if she might determine his intentions. She waited in silence upon her bed, her eyes closed in a feigned attempt to sleep as she counted the moments until they began to run together like sand in a time glass.

Outside her window, the eerie call of an owl echoed through the garden and she started violently in surprise at the sound, searching the corners of the dim room instinctively, but finding nothing. The owl called again, settling her nervousness, but intensifying her desire to discover the source of the presence haunting. She lay back upon her pillow once again. In her noiseless reverie she found her hearing was more attuned to her surroundings, her senses more vigilant. Every whisper of breeze across the emeraldine canopy, every fluttering insect that visited her window and every cry from the forest shook her to her very core. Yet as the night progressed and she struggled against sleep, no ethereal presence crept into her consciousness.

As the first light of dawn speckled the forest with the glimmering light of the sun peeking over the distant horizon Ayla sighed sharply in agitation. Successful only in causing herself undue stress and losing a full night's sleep, she rose wearily from her bed and stared with a bleary gaze out her window as she attempted to focus her thoughts and gather some residual strength to face the coming day. She would not tell anyone of her sleepless night or of her quest to discover the truth about her tormentor, as she had begun thinking of him. Such conversations would only bring her under further scrutiny and would serve no useful purpose. She would simply continue on and hope the next time she sensed *his* presence she would be better prepared to determine the truth about him.

* * *

Summer waned and autumn began to tinge the woodland with shades of gold, crimson and russet, and in response the Fey began preparations for the coming silence of winter. Additional vigilance had to be taken during the long months of wind and brutal weather. Walls that were weak had to be reinforced; roofs that were thin required supplementary thatching; warm, woolen cloaks had to be cleaned and prepared for extended months of use. The flocks of sheep and goats that provided milk, butter, cheese and wool had to be gathered into sheltering barns and stables. Many of the artifacts that graced walkways, byways and gathering groves were removed and stored in secure buildings or covered tightly with waxed, woolen tarps, which would keep out even the most drenching rain or seeking ice.

The nursery gamesyard was also closed down for the season. Toys and entertainments that delighted young Fey the remainder of the year were relocated indoors or covered for the season and the inner gardens where the childfey would play for the next several months were cleaned, refreshed and brightened with torches. Everyone helped to ensure all the necessary changes were ready before the cold hand of frost from the lands of the North descended upon Hwyndarin and this meant that Ayla got to see much of Mardan.

They were often found working together, side by side and vastly contented to be so. They would luncheon together along with Nayina and her companion Reydan. They would tarry in secret avenues of beech coppice in delightful solitude and they would fly hand in hand to Ayla's door nearly every evening, reluctant to part even for the few short hours of the night. Ayla's heart filled with affection for her attentive companion and almost before she could put a name to her own feelings her few close friends were whispering surreptitiously of her being in love.

One late October morning, Mardan found himself detained and unable to meet her before she set off for the nursery gardens where she was helping to decorate the interior walls with intricately folded and cut paper birds, butterflies, and all manner of fauna. They had already painted the walls a rainbow of bright colors and had only these last details to complete to make the gardens appropriately cheerful. Ayla waited on him as long as possible, but in the end had to proceed on her own through the sparse alleyways of pear and pine, and as she fluttered hurriedly through the crisp morning air she felt a tinge of apprehension slither over her.

Immediately she recognized the sensation. She was not alone, although no other Fey were within sight. She was concealed by the pear trees, which had not yet shed their crimson leaves. There were no homes along the way to which she could flee and the nursery was still some distance away. Even her friend Nayina lived too far away; she had no alternative but to stop, turn and face her tormentor.

She knew it was *him* instantly. The spine-tingling sensation of trepidation and inexplicable curiosity that accompanied his presence had become unnervingly familiar. Although she could not ascertain his purpose in pursuing her and she was aware of his presence with startling regularity, he never once fully revealed himself to her. Moreover, she did not mention his 'visits', as she had begun calling them, to either Nayina or Mardan in the fear that they might think her off-balance or notify the Elders. She merely continued to do everything within her power to contain her fright at being thusly pursued and, each time she became aware of him, she made a diligent attempt to pierce the darkness surrounding him.

Turning in the air nonchalantly, she swept her gaze over the surrounding woodland hoping to discover his whereabouts, but his presence was as vague as ever. The misty forest hampered her inspection of her surroundings, yet as she turned back in the direction of the nursery a brief vision arrested her gaze. From the corner of her sparkling amber eyes she could, at last, make him out. Excited and terrified in the same instant, she dared not spin round to face him, but gazed sidelong in overwhelming, trembling curiosity.

She had not been mistaken. He was undeniably malefey. Although he remained cloaked in the shadows, she could see he was tall and was dressed in very dark colors, which was quite odd for a Fey of the Light. Most Fey she knew were fair of aspect, fair of countenance and fairly adorned, yet he pressed into the shadows of the forest and was only barely discernible. Most startling of all was the deep red of his aura.

She could not prevent herself from turning at this shocking discovery to gaze at him directly, yet, in that moment, he vanished into the darkness like a wolf disappearing into fog. Utterly exasperated and unable to contain herself, she cried out after him in the loudest voice she could muster.

"Who are you?" Only silence answered her, but she could not bring herself to shrug him off and continue along her way. She knew he remained, watching her; he had simply concealed himself better.

"What do you want of me?" she called after him again.

From the opposite direction, in a rush of feathers and swirling leaves, she felt a sudden presence come up behind her. Right behind her! Twisting abruptly with a shriek, she backed away, unprepared for such a sudden assault, but even as she turned a familiar voice rang in her ears.

"I am sorry I frightened you, Ay." It was Mardan. He had caught up with her and now hovered over her with an unreadable expression of concern. She jolted backward in surprise, then sighed prodigiously and flung her arms about him.

"Oh it is you, Mardan," she exclaimed and then checked herself. She dared not risk the chance that the one person in the world who she cared about above everything and everyone else should think she was odd. Enough Fey already had that impression. He returned her embrace warmly, pulling away from her slightly to give her a tender kiss in greeting. For a brief moment, her senses spun with dizzy delight and her awareness of *his* presence faded, but when Mardan pulled away and looked upon her with a markedly questioning gaze she knew she had to give some explanation for her peculiar behaviour.

"I did not know who was following me," she explained, attempting to keep her tone as blithe as possible, but her voice quavered in spite of her efforts.

"Should the thought of someone following you distress you so?" Mardan asked, his concerns deepening. He knew there was not a single Fey in all Hwyndarin that she needed to fear and she shook her head and laughed awkwardly.

"Of course not. You just surprised me." Her nonchalant reiteration did not satisfy his intensifying concern and he reached to take her hand, staying her attempt to continue on as if nothing had happened.

"Ayla, you were more than surprised; you screamed."

She paused, unwilling to return his stare. In her sudden discomfort she became aware of his skepticism, as well as the increasing interest of the one still observing her from the shadows.

"Clearly *something* has distressed you. Why will you not tell me what it is?" Mardan's tone was gentle and justifiably anxious, yet she could not contain her sudden resentment of what she thought were unspoken accusations. Flustered by his interrogation, she sighed sharply and spun round to face him.

"Nothing has distressed me. Can I help it if you startled me?" Mardan's eyes widened at her caustic tone, but even her rebuke betrayed her. She had never spoken unkindly to him before or behaved so uncharacteristically cold.

"I suppose not." His vague reply only fueled her fire of suspicion against him. She knew well enough how disparagement felt, but when it came from someone she cared so much about it hurt doubly. "You would tell me if something bothered you, would you not?" he verified, but she only shrugged and offered that she might, which amazed him even more greatly. "Why only might you?" His further inquiry broke her thread of patience and she smacked her delicate wings sharply together in an irrefutable display of anger.

"Because I cannot tolerate the condescension of everyone when they think how odd I am!" she retorted with tears standing in the clear amber of her eyes; then she turned abruptly away and shot off towards the nursery, leaving Mardan behind in a confusion of thoughts and emotion.

A few yards away, secluded in the shadows of the forest and equally perplexed by her sudden display of intense emotion, *he* watched her retreat as well.

Chapter Three

Of course, Ayla could not maintain her anger toward Mardan for long, it was as impossible as refusing to breathe, but, almost imperceptibly, her uncertainty about him began to grow. Slowly, like twilight fading into a moonlit night, she began to doubt the sincerity of his feelings for her. More and more frequently she struggled with the thoughts that he was like all the others, that he held her unusual abilities suspect and that he would eventually grow tired or bored of her, break her heart, and move on. Long nights passed as she tossed and turned in tormented dismay; endless afternoons dragged on like years as she waited for him to visit her or write to her when he was away at the Temple; dark, torturous thoughts haunted her mind, compelling her to make the first move and end things before she could be hurt.

And all the while, the presence of her tormentor haunted her.

"I saw him, Nayina," she confessed one rainy afternoon as they sat quietly watching the little ones in the nursery garden. Certain immediately of whom she spoke without needing to clarify, Nayina jumped in surprise.

"When? Where? What does he look like? Is he handsome? Did you talk to him? Who is he?" Her questions tumbled out in a rush, as if she had been holding them back for months and only now could finally ask them. Ayla shook her head.

"I saw him a few weeks ago. It was the morning Mardan and I fought. He was following me through the pear grove and I turned suddenly and saw him, but only for a moment."

"Did you recognize him?"

Ayla shook her head. "I have never seen anyone like him before." She described the brief vision she had of his appearance and Nayina smiled teasingly.

"No wonder you fought with Mardan!" she implied mischievously, but Ayla was not amused. His visits had become too frequent and he remained silently and invisibly watching her for longer and longer periods of time.

"Mardan and I fought because he thinks I am odd, just as everyone else does and I finally realized it!" she snapped, jumping up from their lounging place to stalk away from her friend towards a nearby, indoor brook that babbled and tumbled through the garden. Nayina gazed after her in surprise, fluttering after her to alight nearby.

"You of all people ought to know exactly and without any shred of doubt how Mardan truly feels about you," she quipped with a hint of irritation. Ayla knew she spoke the truth, but for some reason beyond her own comprehension, her impression of Mardan's affection had become confused by her own fears and doubts. She simply was no longer sure and she could not ascertain the truth from him, either by sense or by word. As a Celebrant, he was separate, aloof, and far more difficult to read than many. Shaking her head, she redirected their conversation back to *him*.

"He did not talk to me, although I tried to make him. He just watched me. It is all the time now, Nayina, and I do not know what to do about it."

Her friend did everything she could to temper her anxiety at hearing this admission before speaking. She knew Ayla could easily misinterpret any measure of concern in her present state of mind. "All the time?"

"Nearly, he never talks to me; he never comes out of the shadows; he is just there, watching and listening."

Nayina contemplated the few facts she knew and then gasped. "Ay, is he a Dark One?" she breathed warily, her voice a whisper in case, even now, *he* observed them. Ayla winced, even though the thought had already occurred to her a hundred times. She turned secretively toward her friend and shook her head.

"Everything I have ever been taught about the Dark Fey does not apply to him, Nay, except that he remains hidden in shadow. He has not tried to hurt me. He has not tried to take any of the children I guard. He has not opened any portals. He is just there. I cannot explain why, but I certainly cannot call him Reviled for that."

Nayina straightened and spoke more authoritatively. "This has gone on long enough. I remember the first time you saw him in the gamesyard and that was months ago. You need to tell someone other than me. You need to at least tell Mardan."

At the mention of Mardan's name Ayla cringed and shook her head. "He already thinks I am peculiar, just like everyone else, but if I told him that some strange malefey has been following me around and watching me for months and I have done nothing about it, he will surely end things. Even worse, he could bring the Elders into the matter and I would be a prisoner again like I was all those years. I just cannot tell him Nayina, and you must promise me that you will not tell him either!"

* * *

For many long weeks Nayina tried to convince her friend of her error of judgment; that Mardan no more thought she was odd than she did, but her success was limited. Too many years of scrutiny had come before. Ayla knew only too well that she was isolated and set apart from her fellow Fey and this knowledge had become a thorn, forever piercing her perceptions. There was little anyone could do now to change that. Ayla struggled with her insecurity daily, whether it related to Mardan specifically or everyone in the village in general. Some days she had very little doubt in her mind of his fondness for her and enjoyed their growing affection immensely; other days it was all she could do to trust even a single word from his mouth.

Ayla never spoke about her misgivings with Mardan. She was fearful of his reaction to that truth and she was unwilling to worsen the situation by verbalizing her doubts. She believed, as most Fey did, that words had nearly limitless power once spoken and believed. She refused to give her foolish inclinations such an advantage over her. Yet, although she made a conscious effort every day to keep her thoughts aligned with the Light, her uncertainties ultimately won out.

As the seasons shifted from autumn to early winter and a shroud of cold darkness began to fall upon the beautiful village of Hwyndarin, the Fey gathered together for one final celebration of color and brightness. They dressed in glittering, bejeweled costumes; decorated their homes with sparkling lanterns carved out of hallowed gourds; carved wooden and pumpkin decorations; filled their porches and gardens with sweet baked treats and sugary indulgences for any passerby to enjoy, and played a multitude of musical instruments in a discordant symphony of joyful sound. Parading along the avenues from home to home in dancing, fluttering, gleeful revelry, Fey of all ages enjoyed the company of their friends and family while eating and drinking the sweet temptations of the season and at the end of the evening's festivities all Fey, young and old, joined together to venerate the passing of the Season of Light.

They gathered in the Clearing of the Stars, where the forest canopy contracted and one could gaze up, out of the forest, into the glittering night sky enchanted by the glowing moon and the sparkling stars overhead. Together, they began the incantation of the changing seasons led by their village Celebrant, their voices subdued and solemn after a full day of laughing and singing. They paced through the intricate dance which marked the ending of the growing and gathering seasons and the beginning of the season of cold darkness with austerity. Bowing, pausing, stepping, clapping, pausing, clasping hands, passing, turning, pausing, releasing, taking to wing, alighting and repeating until the midnight horns rang through the clear, cold night air. The sharp tones signaled more than just the ending of the day; they heralded a somberness that descended upon the village as silently as the first winter snow.

No longer would the days be warm and bright; they would be cold and bleak. No longer would the shushing of emeraldine leaves and the luscious scent of flowers fill the air; there would be only the creaking and groaning of barren branches in the icy gales of winter. No longer would the songs of thrush and cicada ring through the canopy overhead; there would only be silence and the scrunching of snow underfoot. Many months would pass in the uninviting coldness of winter and many Fey would not venture out into the bleakness any longer than their responsibilities required.

Ayla and Mardan, along with Nayina and her companion Reydan, had shared the pleasantries of the evening together. Dressed in complimentary fashion wearing vivid silks, broad hats with bright plumes, jingling bells upon their ankles and trailing streamers from their wings, they had enjoyed their portrayal of jesters completely. Yet now, after the horns sounded, they removed their bells and the instruments that had played all evening fell silent as the Fey returned to their homes in quiet introspection. Bidding their friends a hushed good eventide, Ayla and Mardan turned towards her small cote upon the fringes of the village and Ayla once again felt her isolation. How long would she suffer her loneliness? How long would she remain an outsider among her own people?

Mardan could easily sense the shift in her spirits and when they reached her door, he paused to draw her close in a warming embrace. Long they stood in each other's arms and Mardan did not confuse the pure sentiment of the moment by bending to kiss her, in spite of the hammering of his heart. Rather, he stood quietly and simply held her, completely aware of the trembles coursing through her and uncertain as to their cause or cure. She did not speak, but clung to him like a child in a raging tempest who is frightened by the storm around her and, after many long moments, he pulled away from her.

"Are you alright, Ay?" he asked softly, afraid that his genuine concern might light the increasingly short fuse of her temper, but, instead of becoming irritated, she sighed bitterly and brushed a trail of tears from her cheeks.

"No," she replied miserably. Mardan's concern intensified and he took her small hands in his own.

"Ay, I do not want to upset you and I do not want to argue with you again, but I know something has been troubling you these past weeks. Can we not talk about whatever it is? If I am doing something to offend or displease you, I cannot alter it unless I know what it might be?" He spoke softly and to his surprise, she burst into tears and flung her arms about his shoulders, burying her sadness in his comforting embrace. Tenderly, and without regard to the hour, he led her inside her cottage and closed the door behind them.

Vigilant to refresh the porch lantern with oil and then the many small lamps around her home, he returned to her side in the small parlor only after seeing to these vital tasks, sat down beside her upon the roll-back settee, and encouraged her to tell him what was upsetting her so prodigiously. She tried to contain her emotion so she could speak plainly, but to her dismay she realized she could sense *his* presence.

"Oh, not now," she breathed in exasperation, utterly confounding Mardan, who turned his head to one side and stared at her with a furrowed expression, bewildered.

"What have I done," he asked uncertainly, but Ayla shook her head.

"It is not you, Mardan. You have done nothing wrong. I simply..." she struggled to find the words, but they eluded her. Distracted by the sensation that *he* was unusually close and desperate to be alone in order to discover his intent at long last, she attempted to bounce to her feet, but Mardan caught her wrist and refused to permit her to escape.

"Then why do you treat me this way?" His tone betrayed the weeks of frustration he had suffered while attempting to be patient and understanding. She turned to look at him sadly.

"Mardan, I am sorry, truly I am, but perhaps what everyone says about me is true: perhaps I *am* strange," she explained with resignation, but he shook his head.

"I do not think you are strange. I think you are keeping something from me. I do not know how to prove that you can trust me, but you can, Ayla."

She gazed at him thoughtfully. Should she tell him of her tormentor? Would he understand her reasons for tolerating the long months of *his* visits? Could their relationship survive such a disturbing revelation? She hoped it might, but she was not given time to deliberate further.

"*Ayla.*"

For one brief, horrifying second Ayla heard a whisper that made her jump to her feet, wrench her arm from Mardan's steady grasp and spin round in desperation seeking the source of the sound she had just heard. Mardan watched her transfixed, astonished beyond words by her irrational behavior, but she could not bring herself to stop. The whisper had been so soft, but she had heard it. *He* had clearly spoken her name.

"Did you hear that?" she turned and asked Mardan abruptly. He got to his feet slowly, perplexed as well as curious.

"What did you hear?"

Ayla turned back to gaze out the parlor window, stretching her senses forward like a fisherman casting a net into dark waters. *He* was there, just beyond the margins of the forest; yet he had whispered her name and she had heard it.

"Did you not hear it?"

"Hear what, Ay?"

"My name. It was a whisper, but it was my name, I am sure of it," she exclaimed hurriedly, heedless of how peculiar such a statement sounded. Mardan stood quietly a moment, endeavoring to fathom her suggestion. If she had heard a whisper, then the speaker should have been within the house, within that very room, but she was staring out the window toward the forest. Mardan stepped closer.

"Someone whispered your name from outside?" he asked, clearly puzzled, however when she spun around on her heel to rebuke his disbelief he reiterated swiftly. "Ay, I did not hear anything, but if you heard a whisper, surely it did not come from outside." His attempt to illustrate her actions in some logical context made her pause. Of course, he was correct. She realized how ridiculous she appeared, but she only wanted to seek answers to her many questions about *him* before he disappeared again.

"I must have sensed it," she muttered, half to herself. Mardan raised an eyebrow at this and shook his head, but said nothing more; her conduct simply too baffling to abide.

"You heard nothing?" she asked again, ceasing her restless pacing to gaze up at him, realizing at last how he stared at her with a completely confounded expression. Raising her hands to mollify his obvious irritation, she retraced her steps to him, shook her head and drew a deep breath before delving into a long withheld explanation. "I realize how crazy I must sound."

He did not deny it.

"But I have not told you about *all* of my abilities, mostly because I was afraid you, just as everyone else, would think I am odd."

"Ay, you say that all the time, but I have never heard anyone say anything against you." Mardan contradicted her, but she barely heard him.

"I was chosen to be educated as a Guardian because of my unique abilities; I can perceive truth from lies without hearing a single word; I can ease another's suffering through empathic contact, and I have highly attuned senses far beyond the normal ranges."

Mardan listened with curiosity, but he did not interrupt her progress with the multitude of questions erupting in his mind.

"For several months now I have been aware of a presence, a presence that is not always with me, but comes and goes of its own accord, yet unfailingly returns again and again. I sense when he is present and when he is gone and, although I cannot make him speak to me to tell me why he should be here at all, I have been waiting, trying to determine his purpose and decide upon a proper course of action. Because I was so uncertain, I only spoke to Nayina about it." She fell silent and watched closely as Mardan absorbed all she had just revealed, certain he would shake his head, utter some cruel reference at her expense and take his leave of her, but he only stood quietly and gazed back at her. After several protracted moments, he broke the silence with a single question.

"A presence?"

She nodded.

"A *male* presence?"

She hesitated at his specification, but agreed again.

"A male presence that will not divulge his purpose for intruding upon your privacy, yet whom you allow to continue to do so without inquiry?"

Ayla swallowed hard at this further clarification, but agreed once again. "I know that sounds," she tried to explain herself further, but Mardan's jaw tightened and his brilliant eyes narrowed.

"*Do* you know how that sounds?" He rebuked her with a tone she had never heard in his sweet tenor voice before and she cringed.

"It sounds crazy, which is why I have not told anyone. Everyone thinks I am crazy enough," she spat defensively, but he ignored her justification.

"It sounds very dangerous to me, Ayla." His use of her full name and the soft tone with which he made his statement made her check the hateful thoughts suddenly swirling in her mind and brought her gaze to his. "Who can say what his intentions are? And, Ay, truly, no one thinks you are crazy."

She stared at him, mystified. She had anticipated that he would be angry or, perhaps even jealous, but she never expected him to be, first and foremost, concerned with her welfare.

"I was trying to discover what his intentions are by reading him," she said softly. Mardan insisted that she explain what she meant, yet when she had given him a description of the extraordinary ability she possessed he stepped back from her with a darkening expression.

"You have spent months attempting to 'read' this trespassing, inexplicable stranger, but you mistrust me and fail to confide anything in me when I am here, in the flesh, every day; neither hiding my intentions nor seeking to manipulate you?"

Ayla stared at him, horrified by his clarification of the truth. Hastily, she attempted to explain that she had never quite thought of it that way. She had only hoped to not jump to any unfair conclusions about *him* that might lead him into harm or under scrutiny. She knew how uncomfortable it felt to be analyzed, particularly by the Elders, and she never wished anyone to undergo such an ordeal, regardless of their actions. *He* had never harmed her or given her any indication that he would. She was careful to discern as much through her senses each time she became aware of him and had she felt in any way threatened she would have told someone immediately.

Mardan's opinion, however, could not be swayed, in spite of her verifications that she had used due caution in dealing with the stranger. He felt betrayed by her lack of trust in him, particularly in light of so serious a situation, and he could not be convinced that she would take him into her confidence either now or in the future. His impression of their relationship had been shattered and he told her as much with as even a tone as he could manage while constraining his anger before he turned toward the door.

"Mardan, I am so sorry!" she cried from her heart and he paused and turned back to gaze at her sorrowfully before he pulled the door open and went out into the dimness of the cool night. Ayla watched him go from the empty portal, her heart breaking into a thousand pieces of ice, but she could not blame him for feeling betrayed and angry. She recognized her mistake, though it came too late and there was, now, no way to set things to rights.

Chapter Four

Ayla stood watching the darkness long after Mardan disappeared into it, her heart hammering and her cheeks wet with unrestrained tears. She realized how foolish she had been for so long. She understood why he felt so betrayed and she recognized how dangerous the situation was that she permitted to continue for reasons quite beyond her understanding. Had Nayina confided in her that such happenings were occurring to her, Ayla would instantly have put an end to it through any means possible, yet she realized that she had not given anyone who cared about her the opportunity to end the dangerous situation maligning her.

Why?

As she closed the door and stepped back into the interior, her thoughts became more introspective. What was this fascination she had with her tormentor? Why was she so persistent about discovering *his* intentions for herself without calling on anyone else for aid? What power did *he* hold over her that compelled her to endure *his* repeated visits on her own? Was it simply, as she professed to Nayina, the fact that she did not intend to bring anyone under the scrutiny of the Elders, being entirely familiar with the discomfort of such a circumstance? Was it the undeniable appeal of the unknown that sealed her lips to telling others about *him* and closed her mind to the possibility of harm? Or was there some deeper, darker power controlling her?

Mardan seemed to think so. He seemed to sense a danger that she offhandedly ignored.

As she returned to the settee, her thoughts returned to the brief vision she had of her tormentor and her mind began to spin with the possible details of *his* appearance. Obsessed by her curiosity to know everything about *him* and unable to recognize the peril inherent in such a fixation, she stepped toward the window that looked out over the garden and gazed out, hoping to capture another glimpse of *him*, however fleeting it may be. Yet only dimness and the shifting shadows of the forest met her gaze and, after staring out for what seemed like hours, she came to her senses, shook off her entrancing reverie and decided to go to bed. She could do nothing about Mardan until the morning and she could do nothing about her tormentor until *he* showed himself either physically or in presence once again.

Sleep eluded her, however. She tossed and turned in her bed, then got up to wander the dimly lighted cottage restlessly before returning to her bed to try to rest once again to no avail. The clock in the parlor chimed one, then two, then three before her eyes grew heavy and her mind stopped spinning and it was only when she curled up on her side and snuggled into the downy softness of her pillow that she heard a sound. The sound made her eyes snap open and she sat up in bed to gaze round her uncertainly. Had she dreamt it now as she believed she had dreamt it earlier, or had she heard the softest whisper of her name?

"*Ayla.*"

Unmistakably, her name was whispered once again and she jumped out of her bed and twisted about, searching for the source of the whisper.

"What! What do you want?" she insisted to the cool night breeze, but only silence answered her. Frustrated and exhausted, she growled in exasperation and stalked to the window, shouting out into the darkness without the slightest concern of who might hear her.

"I know you are there. Simply because you hide, does not mean I cannot sense you! Stop this at once! Show yourself or be gone; I grow weary of this game!" An owl hooted sharply at her outcry and fluttered away from the chimney of her cottage. The night was growing colder and the breeze uncomfortable. Spitefully, Ayla muttered under her breath, pulled the window closed, then snapped the shutters closed as well, snickering that if *he* did not wish to show himself she would simply shut *him* out. She repeated this action all around the house until every window stood closed and she felt more secure in her protection. Nodding in satisfaction with her actions, she traced her steps back towards her bed, yet even as she paused to slip beneath the warming blankets, once again, she heard her name in the form of a soft, drawn out, whisper.

"*Ayla.*"

She froze. It was impossible that she could hear *him* now, whispering to her from the forest. Where was *he*? She strained every sense of perception in an attempt to locate *him*, but besides the familiar awareness of *his* presence, she could not pinpoint a specific location where *he* might be hiding in the shadows. Without thinking, she answered *his* call in her mind through thought alone with a silent, yet insistent, 'what! what!' and to her disbelief she received an instantaneous reply.

"*You hear me.*" *His* voice was soft in her mind, yet clear as if *he* were standing beside her whispering in her ear. She started back in surprise and spun around, fully expecting to see *him* there next to her, but she could only see the dimness of the room around her and the flickering lamp glowing softly in the corner.

"What do you want?" She spoke aloud, not fully aware of what was happening. Silence. She repeated herself more loudly, but again received no reply. Standing perfectly still in the middle of her room, she reasoned out the dilemma and then, cautiously, she thought the question to herself as clearly as she could manage while struggling to keep her own sense of skepticism from clouding her mind. She waited, then shook her head at her own foolishness when emptiness and silence was her only response. Grasping at the corner of her blankets, she moved to climb into her bed, so weary she felt dizzy and unfocused, yet she never lay down and she never found sleep.

The answer that filled her mind utterly prevented any phantom of sleep.

The answer that filled her mind was indisputable and terrifying.

The answer that filled her mind was inescapable.

"*You.*"

* * *

"You cannot permit this to continue." Nayina cried after listening patiently to her friend's report the next morning. "You must call on Mardan and explain things to him and you *must* tell the Elders." Nayina was by nature sweet of temperament and jovial, but she would not be resisted in her recommendations and Ayla knew she was right.

They sat beneath a small beech coppice planted in the fertile soil within the indoor garden that made up the winter nursery. Indoors, the plants stayed ever green, ever lush, and the temperature stayed delightful year-round. Childfey giggled and shouted nearby, unaware of the urgent, desperate conversation taking place so close to them. They scampered and dashed in and out of the garden thickets entirely immersed in contented play. Around them, the soothing sound of splashing waters softly echoed and the babbling brook that meandered throughout the garden supplied a constant undertone of peaceful suspirations.

"I know, Nay. I cannot imagine why I resisted before, but surely I must tell someone." Ayla had never felt so afraid in her life, but not that *his* answer rung clearly in her mind, she could not deny her fear. She had never understood the paralyzing weight of dread, nor comprehended the confusion of sheer panic, but she knew them well now. It had been too late and too dark to escape her small cottage when the answer she had sought for so long filled her thoughts and she had been forced to endure the torturous silence and darkness of the night entirely alone. In her fear, she had lighted every candle and lantern she owned and spoken spells of protection about herself without ceasing until sunlight broke through the dark woodland of Hwyndarin. Then, in the safety of Light, she had flown with the speed of a falcon stooping from a great height to her only friend and confidant.

"I should go and find Mardan. He will know what to do." Nayina suggested, but Ayla grasped her friend tightly by the arm, too afraid of being on her own to allow her to leave. She convinced her to remain until teatime, the hour of four, when the wee Fey tots she guarded would be collected by their parents and she could then accompany her friend to go in search of Mardan. Until that time, they spoke in hushed tones about her tormenter and *his* horrifying revelation.

"Surely he is a Dark One, why else would he hide in the shadows?" Nayina said softly, unsure if *he* was nearby even then, watching them and listening. Ayla shook her head.

"Honestly, I am not sure about that. I have guarded little ones on many occasions and *he* has never once threatened any of them. Besides, do not forget that I have seen *him* twice during the daytide." Ayla reminded her friend, still defensive, although she no longer felt any shred of security in *his* presence.

"You know as well as I do, Ay, that Dark Ones do not always come for children and though you have seen him in the light, he has always been surrounded by shadows. If he is not one of the Reviled, I shall shun flight for a year!" Nayina rebuked her assuredly and her friend had no counter. She was right, of course; Nayina had been right since the very first time she had seen *him*: a mere shadow in the surrounding green woodland beside the gamesyard of the nursery. How long ago that seemed! Indeed, it was months ago, nearly half a year, and Ayla shuddered to think how long she had permitted *him* to trespass into her privacy and threaten her safety.

"I am so ashamed of how I have treated Mardan. I can never forgive myself for being so cold to him, for neglecting him so. He has always so good to me, always so gentle and sweet. Oh Nay, do you think he can forgive me? Do you think he will ever even speak to me again?"

"He will." Came her answer, but it was not Nayina's voice. It was a male voice, softly spoken from somewhere behind her and the sound instantly terrified her. The possibility that her tormenter was suddenly upon them was more than she could bear. Ayla shrieked in fear, blindly flinging herself into the protective embrace of her friend.

"Ayla, it is alright!"

Ayla heard the words, but fear held her in its icy grasp like the death grip of a raptor upon its prey. She could scarce draw breath. She could not turn around to dare a glimpse at the unknown presence behind her, and she could not restrain her tears of dismay. Trembling from head to toe to wingtip, she pressed into her friend's embrace begging her to speak a spell of protection before it was too late, desperate to protect them as well as the children who now stood staring a short distance away.

"I cannot speak it, Nayina," she squeaked timidly, "Speak our protection!"

"Ay, we are safe. Look and see."

She could not. She gasped for breath, but her lungs burned; she attempted to rise to her feet, but her knees were weak with fear and panic.

"Ayla. Do not be so afraid." The male voice seemed a long distance away, echoing strangely in her head and an odd rushing sound, much louder than the brook babbling nearby, rang in her ears. She felt arms encircle her, she felt Nayina release her, but her terror trapped her. Blackness swirled heavily up from the pit of her stomach and the last thing she saw were cerulean eyes gazing worriedly into hers.

When she awoke, she was in a quiet room aglow with soft lantern light and the flickering glimmer of firelight. She lay upon a divan with a pillow beneath her head and a soft blanket covering her. The nursery was gone, the children were gone and the rushing sound in her head was gone. She groaned and attempted to rise, but her head spun like a top and she lay back, utterly dazed. Where was she?

"Nayina?" she whispered cautiously and to her relief her friend answered.

"Right here," she said from behind her, "and someone else too."

Ayla tried to twist round to see, but then Mardan stepped quietly to her side and smiled, crouching down beside the divan and taking Ayla's hand gently.

"I never meant to scare you so, Ay," he apologized softly, his piercingly blue eyes locked upon her. "Nayina has explained why you were so afraid though, so you only need rest. We can talk later."

Ayla smiled and shook her head. "Mardan, I am so sorry." Her voice was a thread, but his heart heard all it needed to hear. Nayina stepped quietly from the room and left them to speak in privacy, a well pleased smile upon her face and a furrow of deep-rooted concern wrinkling her brow.

"Mardan, we must speak now," Ayla insisted, pushing herself up from the comfort of the divan with urgency in spite of his insistence that she should rest. "*He* could come for me at any time."

"This 'tormenter'?" Mardan attempted to keep up with her shifting thoughts. She nodded, then grimaced.

"I cannot forgive myself, Mardan. I was so cold to you all this time and you have been so good to me. I cannot even imagine what you felt last night or how you could bring yourself to come see me today." She flung herself into a long overdue apology, but Mardan shook his head.

"Hush, Ay, it is all right now."

She did not even hear him. "You have been kinder to me than anyone ever has, even from the moment we met," she plunged on. Mardan took her trembling hands in his and shook his head.

"Ayla, stop. There is no need." His soft assertions did not lessen the burden of guilt she carried. She attempted to continue on undeterred, but he leaned closer and pressed his lips to hers, silencing her with a tender kiss.

"There is an end to it, now," he said with finality and she smiled dimly and relented. "You must rest, for as I understand it you have not slept well in many long weeks."

Ayla attempted once again to argue her point, but he raised his hand and gently pressed his fingers to her lips.

"I shall hear no argument, Ay. Rest well, knowing that you are well guarded here in my home with both friend and faithful attendant watching over you and we shall speak upon the morrow." Then he stood, not allowing her a moment to counter his demand, and moved quietly away from her, closing the door partially behind him as he went out.

Relief flooded over her like a spring torrent and she could not resist the tears that came rushing over her. For many long moments she sat quietly, ashamed of her behavior and thankful beyond words for Mardan's forgiving and gentle nature. She felt secure in the knowledge that she was being vigilantly guarded and closed her eyes with a sensation of peace she had not experienced in many months. Sleep stole over her and she rested deeply for many hours, waking at last during the darkest part of the night.

Glancing around her with a tinge of suspicion, she saw that the room glowed softly from night lanterns and Nayina dozed quietly only a few feet away. Mardan was not in the room, but she smiled, fully aware that he was close by. Stretching like a well-rested cat, she righted herself and stepped quietly to the window, cracking the shutters slightly to peer curiously outside. The moon shone brightly through the vale dropping shadowy silhouettes to the forest floor and a chill breeze blew, but the night was clear and bright. Ayla breathed deeply. She could smell winter on the air and the crisp, clean scent made her smile and dream about the pleasant moments between herself and Mardan yet to come, of sharing fires beneath a hearth and warming cups of tea; of spending long hours reading softly to each other, and of even sweeter moments.

Her smile faded sharply as the clock in the corner tolled two and her keen senses detected a frighteningly familiar presence. Even here among her attentive friends her tormentor stole secretly upon her privacy and witnessed her actions in rapt silence. She turned warily, seeking *him* through thought alone, closing her eyes to the comfortable environs surrounding her to sharpen her awareness of *him*. She vividly recalled *his* haunting whisper in her mind and the terrifying answer she had received only hours before, yet in spite of her fear, she now felt even more curious about *him* than before.

If *he* had meant to harm her, surely *he* would have already done so. *He* had had ample opportunities. The answer *he* had given had sent shards of icy terror through her; nevertheless, *he* had not then, nor did *he* now attempt to make any move against her and it was this consistency in *his* behavior that compelled her to seek further and question deeper. She knew she could not speak aloud to gain her answers. If Nayina or Mardan overheard they would never understand, so, instead, she cleared her mind of fear and twisting thought and focused on *his* presence.

Sitting down in an armchair located in the far corner of the room where the dim light from the night lantern only barely reached her, she closed her eyes once again and stretched forth her senses. *He* was close, much closer than she had ever felt *him* before, although she could still not pinpoint *his* precise whereabouts. Whether *he* was within the same room or just on the other side of the wall or ceiling, she felt as if *he* stood directly beside her and she could not still a tremor from running through her, although if it came as a result of fear or in answer to agitation or excitement she could not determine.

"Who are you?" she thought with perfect clarity, anticipating an instant reply, however only silence filled her mind. She repeated her query, unsuccessfully. Opening her eyes with frustration, she puzzled over the situation, trying to figure *him* out. *He* was there, right there, still *he* did not respond to her. Why? She mused for many moments; then straightened as an unbidden thought entered her mind. Perhaps she was not asking the right question. She swallowed with renewed determination and closed her eyes yet again, refocusing herself.

"Do you want to speak to me?" Her mind filled with the question; then emptied, like ripples on a pond.

"*Yes*," the soft, prolonged whisper came softly in reply. She shuddered and smiled at the same time. The sound was deep, distinctly male. It was frightening, yet alluring; the connotations of *his* answer set her nerves on edge, yet melted through her like one of Mardan's gentle kisses. She shivered at the thought and concentrated harder on the moment at hand.

"I am here, listening." She filled her thoughts with the words once again, like a rock thrown into a still pool with circles of rings rippling outward, slowly fading. She waited for many moments, remaining centered, unwilling to break the thread of the moment by either moving or opening her eyes.

"*Alone.*" The reply was softer, stretched out like an echo, yet she understood *him* perfectly. *He* would not speak to her now; *he* would not give evidence of himself under the close scrutiny of her friends. *He* would wait until she was once again safely alone and only then explain himself. She knew all of this without a single additional word from *him* just as she also knew that *he* was only there, now, giving her proof of *his* continued presence because she asked for it. She knew *he* would wait until the moment of *his* choosing and there was nothing further to be gained at that moment.

Opening her eyes to the present moment, she sighed deeply and relaxed into the chair. She felt quite drained from her telepathic endeavors, far more so than when she relied upon her empathy alone, yet it seemed this form of communication was *his* only choice or option. She suddenly yearned for sleep, but even as she retraced her steps to the divan, she decided to visit the village library on the morrow and learn more about the ancient art of telepathy.

Chapter Five

Days passed in silence without another word from *him* and Ayla began to wonder if she had simply imagined speaking with *him* in her mind, the conversation a fabrication of her own exhaustion and mental depletion. She had been neglecting her meditating for weeks while seeking answers. She had strayed from reading the ancient passages that always gave guidance and direction to her, otherwise, disordered life. She had given herself over to the present only, forgetting about the immortal inside her, around her, and had lost her way. The secretive search for answers to questions she barely knew how to ask had led her far from the teachings and training she had received year after year in the Temple and she knew there was only one course of action left to her.

With Mardan beside her she retraced her path. They spent quiet days together in the early winter light reading the ancient texts, meditating on the Light, balancing spirit, aura, and breath to find healing and renewal and, as a natural consequence of this time spent centering themselves on what was fundamentally important, their own relationship was rekindled. They spent long hours sitting in flickering candlelight talking quietly about nothing important or about the upcoming season of scarcity and the preparations, which were already being undertaken, for Years Long Night. They shared their dreams for the future, a future shared together, and Mardan's attentiveness grew increasingly affectionate and tactile. His whispers became more frequent and the intense, long silences that stretched between them filled with a tension Ayla had never experienced before.

They planned a special evening together to be alone for the first time and Ayla could not help wondering if he would make the night special in ways other than with words alone. She knew he was a warm, devoted Fey by nature, but devotion only lasted so long without the joining of heart, soul and body. It was something she had been schooled about, something she had studied in the Temple, but she never anticipated it was something that would come to her. She felt entirely unprepared and nervousness fluttered in the pit of her stomach for hours before the time they had agreed to meet; still, it was not anxiety alone. During the past several days she had come to understand her feeling for her dearest Mardan and had realized how selfish she had been for so long. This was the night she intended to show him just how much he truly meant to her. This was the night she chose to unfold her wings and fly freely with him.

The moon was full as it rose over the lip of the crimson horizon, the hours of twilight fading into the deeper shades of night. Evening breathed softly, shadow and starlight melting together under the canopy of barren branches and dusky pine boughs. Winter was stealing ever closer upon leaden feet leaving frost and glazings of ice in its wake. The night grew colder; the fire beneath the mantle grew ruddier, and the glimmering face of the Queen of the Night rose higher in the sky surrounded by crimson clouds that reflected her pale glare.

Ayla stood waiting in the center of her parlor for Mardan's distinctive knock to sound lightly upon her front portal. She had filled her cottage with candles, their soft glow flickering and dancing around her like the flutters wheeling inside her and she stretched out her senses to seek him, anticipation dancing through her. In her hands, she toyed absently with a blushing, copper rose, which Mardan had given to her the day before as a token of his undying love, yet without warning it fell to the floor and she stood, transfixed.

She sensed a male presence coming closer and, indistinct as it was being still some distance away, she knew without a shred of misgiving that it was not Mardan. The presence she sensed was stronger, darker, more unrelenting than his devoted, gentle, occasionally mischievous temperament. The essence she touched with her mind was insistent and not to be trifled with on any account. She knew who she touched and she shuddered, though not from fear.

It was *him*.

Ayla glanced round her with sudden apprehension, her thoughts settling over the amount of light within her small cottage. If there was too much light *he* would be forced to stay outside. If there was too little light her safety would be compromised. Then she frowned, aware of, for perhaps the first time, the lucid decision she was making to set her own safety aside where *he* was concerned and she shuddered again, but shook her head. With or without enough light,

Mardan was already on his way to meet her, so her safety was not an issue. He would protect her.

Closing her eyes, she cast her senses outward like blowing out a candle and watching the smoke extend in all directions from the source. She sought to touch *him* once again, seeking an answer to the question that had been tumbling in her mind since their last encounter, regardless of the amount of time she had spent attempting to quell her thoughts in ancient readings. She touched other creatures briefly, disengaging almost instantly after discerning that the thoughts she sought were not there. Doe stealing quietly through undergrowth; a vixen crying under the moon in search of her mate; the nightly sojourning owl fluffing its feathers against the cold; all quiet, all innocent, none coming closer to her.

Then her thoughts touched a dark, brooding, ethereal presence. She gasped in surprise at the fervor of emotion that washed over her mind and stepped back in response to the pounding, breathless onslaught. Her eyes snapped open and she stood in astonished silence, her mouth falling slightly agape as she realized the one she touched was not who she thought. The passion and yearning that surrounded her had a focal point. It was Mardan whom she touched and he was thinking about her!

"*Ayla.*"

Unexpectedly, her mind filled with a low, drawn out whisper; the deep baritone of the speaker frighteningly familiar and she gasped again, louder than before.

It was *him.*

"Oh, not now," she cried out into the hush of her small home, but the persistent answer came back all too quickly.

"*Now, Ayla.*" The whisper was so close, the thought piercing her mind as if *he* stood mere inches away from her and she swayed under the potency of *his* presence, her lashes fluttering.

"Where?" she thought, seeking *him*, but not finding *him*. How could *he* be so close and, still, not be inside the cottage? *He* was closer than ever before. Once again, *his* reply to her question was instantaneous.

"*Here.*" *His* deep voice echoed in her mind, but she opened her eyes just the same, searching her parlor, expecting to see *him* at last; but her two-dimensional thinking brought insidious laughter to the edges of her consciousness and she shook her head at her own folly. Fool! She thought, admonishing her own simplicity.

"Here inside my mind?" she inquired, almost in disbelief and once more the answer came back to her so quickly it seemed *he* was capable of reading her thoughts before she could even think them.

"*Yes.*" *His* answer seemed two-fold and she knew *he* had heard her question as well as her musings. It was evident that *he* was just as gifted as she, even if *he* was a Dark One, and the thought made her shake her head. It was something she had never considered before. Was it possible that The Reviled had their own set of gifts, just as the Light loving Fey did and, if so, why had this truth been hidden from her by the Elders?

Laughter once again echoed in her mind. *He* was laughing at her, and *his* mockery set her on the defensive.

"You find my contemplations amusing?" she thought caustically while she stretched her senses out, ever further, ever deeper, seeking.

"The Elders have not taught you everything." The connotation of *his* dark tone was undeniable and she cringed, though she knew *he* was not there in the same room with her waiting to snatch her up as the Reviled were reported to do. The Dark Fey were said to do many things to torment those of the Light, although she felt neither tormented nor afraid.

He whispered her name again and it was as if she could feel *his* breath against her neck from leaning close to her. "*Ayla.*"

She shivered, her eyes closing, her head tilting back in spite of her uncertainty. She felt *his* presence spreading within her, around her, far and yet near, hovering, waiting, lurking, and she could not restrain the smile that turned her lips. Her heart hammered as she began to understand. *His* presence became so strong she actually raised her hands to touch *him*, certain that *he* stood before her enwrapping her with *his* wings, but only the cool night air met her touch.

"He is coming," he said urgently. "Send him away."

Ayla's eyes flew wide and she gazed round her desperately, unwillingly. "I cannot. Please do not ask it of me." She spoke out loud, her tone betraying the emotion within her, but *his* reply came back, resolute.

"*Send him away.*"

She shook her head, her heart hammering. She did not want to send Mardan away, she wanted what they had planned; she wanted to share the nighttide with him. "You cannot understand," she began, but she never finished. At once, every candle in her parlor guttered and extinguished itself, without a breath of wind or wing, and she was left standing in absolute darkness. She shrieked in surprise, yet before she could take any further action or speak her own protection, which she had been trained to do since the age of three, she heard a sudden rush of wing beats surround her.

"*Do not defy me.*"

The voice in her mind was intractable, vexed. She shrank from *him*, even though she stood alone in her parlor. "He is a Celebrant," she said out loud, "You cannot stay while he is here. *You* must be the one to go." Silence met her words, then, although how it was accomplished was beyond her understanding, every candle that had blown itself out was rekindled. The thunderous wing beats disappeared and, with them, *his* dominating presence; nevertheless, even as she straightened to hear Mardan's rhythmic knock upon her door, *his* voice filled her mind.

"*I will be waiting.*"

* * *

The nighttide had been far more beguiling than she ever dreamed it might be and Ayla could not contain the joy flooding over her, through her, out from her. Her aura brightened under the influence of her new found happiness and all who saw her or spoke with her understood that something had changed, although she never shared with them the reason for the alteration. She shared her secret with the only person who would appreciate it most, her best friend and confidant, Nayina, and they talked for long hours while tending the childfey in the nursery; not in dark detail or vulgar language, but about the love that burst forth from her for Mardan. She shared as well the inconceivable sensation of sharing his emotion; a gift Nayina wished she, too, could experience. For days they whispered, smiled, giggled, never telling another soul, and Nayina never gave the least impression of her knowledge when Mardan would come to visit his love.

Yet in all their conversations and walks along the indoor riverlet, Ayla never once shared the truth about what had occurred before Mardan's arrival. She locked away the sensation of dizziness and rhapsody that had rushed over her when *he* had filled her mind. She dared not admit the truth, even to herself. A truth that could destroy everything she had waited so long to enjoy, a truth that would lead her in a direction she never considered traveling. Nevertheless, the inescapable certainty haunted her day and night.

Whether she went through her daily routine of preparation or traversed the distance from her cottage to the Nursery or sat in Mardan's loving embrace by the fireside sharing their growing fondness, the inexorable fact remained. She had enjoyed the touch of *his* mind. *His* thoughts were as delicious to her as Mardan's and nothing could alter this reality. She could not deny it and she could not continue to ignore it.

Something had to be done.

She spent many nights in seclusion, opening her mind, waiting, inviting, but *he* did not return to her and the silence of *his* absence was nearly more than she could bear. She went for long walks alone in the wintering woods, whispering her presence in her mind and her willingness to listen to *him*, but still, *he* did not come to her. She stretched out her thoughts, over and over, desperate to find *him*, but only the wild creatures of the forest were there.

Time stole by on leaden feet and life returned to what it had been before her first encounter with *him*, yet, in spite of the growing intimacy of her relationship with Mardan, she could not deny the truth.

She missed *him*...

Chapter Six

The forests of Jyndari were vast and Hwyndarin was set nearly in the heart of the ancient woodland. This was done with good reason. On the coast, storms and high winds could sweep in from the oceans or roll off the heights of the Trynnari Mountains and threaten both the stability of essential Light and the equally indispensable treasures of learning collected through the ages, but deep in the center of the primordial forest storms were seldom a threat or even a consideration. Hwyndarin had been chosen millennia ago as the seat of all learning and artistry for this especial reason, for in its protected libraries the precious tomes from thousands of years of wisdom could be housed safely and amid the Temple halls and community gathering places the artisan's treasures could be protected. Yet infrequently, a significantly powerful tempest would press back the borders of the forest and shatter the tranquility of the peaceful village.

The late November day had been extraordinarily fair, but the night brought with it gales and pouring icy rain of unparalleled fury that tore at the canopy above Hwyndarin like a leviathan running its hand over a field of wheat. Boughs and branches crashed down on the village rooftops, rain pelted down like daggers in blinding torrents, and blazing bolts of jagged lightening with resounding clangors of thunder tore the sky repeatedly asunder.

Ayla was guarding the infant of a family called away in grief over the loss of a loved one and had been enjoying a peaceful evening in the quiet solitude of her home with the child. Now, as a bellow of thunder shook her small cottage and the hammering of rain pounded on the rooftop, she held the child close in her arms. She hushed his wailing with a soft, melodic tune, but a furious gust of air blasted open the shuttered windows and shredded her voice. Instantly, her glowing home was pitched into darkness as the gale extinguished every lantern and the child's shriek of fear mimicked her own.

Her thoughts spun in a panic. A mirror stood in darkness in her boudoir, the child's crib room lay in shadows, and the corridor along which she had to travel to reach either held no window, only darkness that could conceal The Reviled, but she knew she had to light at least a single candle and she had to brighten the mirror immediately. Each second it stood in blackness was an opportunity for crossing. Racing to the nearest cabinet, she fumbled with the beeswax taper she found there and whispered one of many, simple spells she used frequently in her daily life.

"Luxay," she said in a commanding tone and the wick popped into flame. The room flickered between shadow and light, yet, it was only a single candle. Should she light more or should she race to the mirror? *A mirror left in darkness cries out to be crossed.* The recitation she had repeated for years in her youth played over and over in her mind, but she could not risk entering a room with a darkened mirror while holding a baby in her arms, ripe for the taking. She was a Guardian; her first duty was to protect the innocent.

Clutching her candle, she drew a deep breath, kissed the tot's head reassuringly and darted along the hall toward his crib room. A small lantern stood upon his night table. She only needed to reach it and light it in order to keep him safe. She stopped at the darkened doorway and peered inside, her sight piercing the ebon shades and her own glimmering aura lending illumination. Stepping into the dark interior, she reached for the lantern, yet even as she touched its cool, brass sheath a shadow contracted in the far corner of the room and she froze in instinctive terror.

The shadow grew darker, denser, then spread outward into the dimness of the room not brightened by Ayla's small candle. Roshwyn in her arms squealed and began to cry louder and she cradled him more tightly, protecting him with her diaphanous wings as her mind spun in alarm.

Light the lantern! Speak the words of protection! Flee!

It was too late.

A Dark One stepped out of the shadows and glared at them with ophidian eyes. The flame in her hand guttered and threatened to go out, but she had no other means of protecting it than repeating her lighting spell with a timorous tone. Shadow swirled about the Dark One like smoke curling around embers and she watched in perfect dread as he slowly reached out his hand toward them.

Light the lantern! Speak the words of protection! Flee!

Years of training screamed at her from within the spiraling depths of her mind, but fear held her transfixed. He stepped closer, his dark eyes glimmering in the fluttering light of her candle, his hand outstretched toward them, toward the child. Light the lantern! Speak the words of protection! Flee!

"Luxay!" Ayla turned toward the lantern and shouted her lighting spell, gasping in relief when the wick snapped into flame, but the Dark One flexed his immense wings and directed a current of air across the room that extinguished both flames, the one she held and the one inside the lantern, in the same moment. Roshwyn screamed and Ayla jerked backwards toward the door, but in an instant, the Dark One was upon them and she stood, paralyzed by dread, as her aura shrank to a feeble glimmer in her terror. The Dark One stared down at her with unreadable crimson eyes, then reached for the squalling child.

"Do not take him," she pleaded, her voice a mere thread. Remarkably, the Dark One paused, regarding her with his snake-like gaze, but the wailing child could not be ignored. He raised his hand once more and uttered a single word in the vile Dlalth tongue, the language of The Lost.

"Gvyndlal."

Ayla stared at the Demonfey standing before her with utter surprise. As Roshwyn's wailing subsided and his squirming ceased, she shook her head and struggled to translate the word he had spoken. Gvyndlal? Sleep? The Dark One had said only 'sleep'?

"Sleep?" She gazed down at the quiet babe in her arms in amazement, then back at the Dark One still glowering over them. Her aura expanded, illuminating his dark silhouette and she beheld for the first time one of The Reviled.

Easily six feet tall, he dwarfed her diminutive stature by at least fourteen inches and had a lithe, powerfully muscular physique. His shoulder length hair was the color of shimmering ice, both white and silver. He wore a full-length coat with burnished gold lacings and buttons, with armor-like plates embellishing his broad shoulders and with dark crimson and vibrant silver silk accentuating the deep lapels of the coat he wore open across his broad chest. The multiple belts and chokers crisscrossing his close fitted vest, his pants and boots were black leather with similar burnished gold fittings and, although she never would have imagined a Dark One dressing so strikingly, he wore a double flounced cravat and golden choker with an enormous ruby glimmering from its heart.

His vast dragonhide pinions were deep black and blood-red, stretching fully twice his height in length, yet with vicious spines at each joint and tip they seemed even larger and were hideously frightful to behold. His complexion was the unmistakable sallow pallor of the Reviled.

"Put the child in his crib," he said unexpectedly, his calm baritone voice sending a violent shiver through her. She hesitated. If she released Roshwyn, he would be lost.

"Put the child in his crib," the Dark One repeated in a more imposing tone. Ayla jolted into motion, but shook with uncontrolled fear.

"Please, do not take him," she whined piteously. The Dark One scowled at her impatiently and stepped closer, pointing insistently at the small cot in the corner of the room. She shuddered visibly at his nearness and shrank away, wholly intimidated by him, but he did something Ayla never would have anticipated. He stepped past her towards the doorway and glanced out into the ebon darkness of the cottage.

"Light your candle, speak your protections and leave him in his cradle," he insisted through gritted teeth, urgency marking his every word. She stared at him perplexed, but only for a moment. Turning to look down upon Roshwyn, she relit her small candle, as well as the lantern, and began her intonation of protection. The words and light made the Dark One step out into the shadows of the hall, as if they sickened him, but they did not banish him back to the realm of Uunglarda as she had always thought they would. When she finished, Ayla turned with a knife of uncertainty twisting in her stomach, but before she had time to consider her next actions, he lunged into the room, grasped her by the wrist and drew her out into the dark corridor.

She recognized her folly immediately. In striving to protect the child, she had unwittingly sacrificed herself. In the darkness of the hall, as he dragged her unfalteringly toward the only room in her home containing a mirror, she recalled the dire warnings given to all young Fey as they entered youth. A mirror never stood in a sleeping chamber for a mirror could never be left in darkness. Should a Dark One cross over, he would open the portal the mirror provided and summon his Legion. Then they would cross in untold numbers visiting such vile acts upon the young Fey as could never be named. They would only return into their own realm when the first light of the sun crossed the horizon, leaving ruination and despair in their wake and, oftentimes, death.

"No!" she shrieked in absolute horror, straining against his grasp, leaning away from him, scratching at his hand, beating her wings with every ounce of strength she possessed, but her resistance seemed more an inconvenience to him than a problem. Tugging her along behind him, he strode purposefully into her boudoir, her private chamber of preparation, and turned toward the mirror. Raising his free hand toward the reflecting glass, he arched his wings as if setting himself against a foe and closed his eyes, beginning an incantation that was not spoken in the Dlalth tongue, but in an arcane language she did not immediately recognize.

Where were all the spells of protection she had learned as a child? How could she have forgotten after repeating them, literally, thousands of times until she was weary of speaking? Her mind spun; her terror choked her; her breath came in ragged gasps; she shook like a willow in a November wind, but she could still hear him speaking in the mysterious language and, in spite of her fear, she could not prevent the shred of curiosity that made her pause and glance up at him. She realized in that brief moment of clarity that his hand around her wrist was not an iron of restriction, clamped around her like a manacle. In fact, astonishingly, he was not hurting her at all.

The mirror creaked like ice shifting on a frozen river, the sound making her tremble more fiercely. He was opening the portal. Desperation inundated her like a spring flood and she pulled against his restraining grasp more vehemently, but he did not even turn his head. Hauling her up against his side, he crossed his arm over her shoulders and pinned her against him, turning the edge of one broad wing toward her furious thrashings to threaten any further resistance with a glinting, ten-inch spine.

Suddenly, her training returned to her and words of protection filled her mind. She gasped them out in haste, but her voice was little more than a choked squeak. Regardless of the weakness in her chanting however, his reaction was instantaneous. Pausing in his invocation, he turned his head to look down at her with obvious irritation, pressed the cruel barb on his wing to the soft skin under her chin and raised his hand from her shoulder to cover her mouth. There was nothing more she could do to protect herself. She had been defeated in her first and only battle. She knew she was utterly lost.

Turning back to the mirror, he began again; the unrecognizable words ringing in her ears like chimes spinning her senses. She was falling under his spell. She was unable to struggle, unable to speak her own protection, unable to do anything other than listen as he opened the portal and wrought her destruction. Yet even in her panic-stricken state, she could not prevent her overly inquisitive mind from lucidly noting that his hand, pressed over her mouth, was not hurting her. He did not bruise her lips under the ferocity of his contact; he did not wrench her head backward with cruel disregard; he did not restrict her breathing. He was simply thwarting her ability to speak.

Why was he being so shockingly careful about not hurting her? Why had he permitted her to protect Roshwyn with Light as well as spell? Why had he pulled the nursery door closed quietly before proceeding to drag her down the hallway toward the mirror? She could not comprehend his entirely incongruous behavior. Moreover, she had always been told The Reviled were cold-blooded, heartless creatures; that the touch of a Dark Fey was icy as death itself, yet, pressed up against him as she was, his warmth was surprisingly undeniable.

The mirror creaked more loudly, drawing her back to the horror of her present situation and, with these calamitous musings confusing her thoughts, she strained to see around his vast pinions and broad shoulders to watch the mirror with morbid curiosity.

Tiny shards like crystalline ice were stretching across the reflective pane, each splinter a minuscule prism that reflected any spark of light in the room, even the ineffectual glimmer of her diminishing aura and his ethereal, dark crimson glow. With each word he spoke, the crystals increased, growing in number, dimension and intensity until they spread across the glass like frost on a winter window. Scraping and creaking like snow scrunching underfoot on the coldest day, the shards in the mirror began to reflect their own luminosity and, as he continued to speak, the luster of the mirror intensified.

Then the mirror resounded with a deafening crack and she flinched abruptly away, a sharp cry escaping her muffled mouth. Even the Dark One recoiled from the force of the sound and fell silent. Petrified, she squeezed her eyes tightly closed and held her breath. He had opened the portal; his kind would soon rush in and then she would pray for death long before it would come. In her terror, she could not breathe, blackness swirled at the edges of her mind, and her knees grew weak. Almost imperceptibly, she began to collapse, sliding down the length of his strong frame with no measure of power left within her to break her fall.

Without a sound, the Dark One turned his head to look down at her and released her. He did not drop her or throw her to the floor like a worn-out plaything; he took her by the shoulder and by the hand and lowered her to the floor at his feet. Her thoughts swirled at this additional peculiarity and, before she lost herself to fear completely and was swallowed up by blackness, she opened her eyes to peer up at him wanly, utterly bewildered.

The room was bathed in Light! The mirror was intact, not lying in a multitude of shattered pieces on the floor as she had expected, and, somehow, it stood aglow with radiant, incandescent Light that sparkled and reflected in its own shimmering! Blinking woozily in the brilliance, she gazed up at him and drew a deep breath.

What had he done?

Chapter Seven

The terror wrenching in the pit of her stomach dissipated and, with it, the swirling blackness threatening to overwhelm her. Slumped on the floor at his feet, she gaped up at the Dark One in dumbstruck silence, every incantation of protection she had ever learned dissolving into nothingness like the fear inside her. What had he done? The words tumbled over and over in her mind as he stood over her quietly, his dark pinions pulled back from their formerly aggressive inclination, revealing his countenance more clearly.

In the bright, shimmering light pouring from the shattered mirror, she realized that her previously hasty examination of him had been tainted by fear. He was certainly a Dark One, there was no mistaking that truth; his hair was the oddest colour of silvery white, his clothes were the colour of pitch, and his vast, leathery wings were barbed with cruel points; nonetheless, there was something about him that she could not disregard.

Lifting one hand slowly to shield his crimson gaze from the cascading light spilling from the mirror, he looked down at her with a devilish grin turning the corners of his mouth and she could not keep herself from starting back in renewed horror, certain that his intentions were as dark and fearsome as he was, but rather than grab her roughly and haul her to her feet or speak callously to her as she anticipated he would, he only turned his head slowly to gaze at the mirror and plainly consider his handiwork.

The mirror stood intact, yet in a myriad of shattered pieces held intact within its bright glass. No longer creaking like ice shifting on a frozen river, it pierced the room with incandescent light that illuminated every corner. How had he achieved this remarkable accomplishment? She had never seen such in her lifetime; she had never even heard of such being done, and yet, as she stared at the shimmering glow, her mind turned the question over again and again... What had he done?

"I closed the portal," he answered simply, his deep baritone voice suddenly familiar to her. Her glimmering gaze caught his and she stared at him, unable to speak; her thoughts tumbling in confusion and recognition as she came to the unanticipated realization that he was the one who had been whispering to her for months, following her every move, tormenting her with his silent presence: *Him*.

He turned his head to gaze down at her once again, his smile broadening as his voice filled her mind, although he never opened his mouth. *"Hello Ayla."* The manner in which he spoke to her in a drawn-out whisper sent a shiver down her spine, but she could not stop the smile that curved her lips any more than she could restrain herself from staring at him in utter astonishment.

Like a mirage that twisted and warped under the glow of the sun, his physical appearance changed now that he was standing in the Light and now that she did not look upon him with insurmountable dread. In the shadows he had drawn around himself before shattering the mirror, his every aspect reflected darkness. His hair, his eyes, his jet colored clothes, even his aura, but now, bathed in shimmering light, she saw an entirely different person. Like a chameleon, he seemed to shift with the light.

He laughed at her musings, turning to look at her more closely as she struggling to get to her feet and to her utter surprise, he reached out to assist her, his hand offered palm up in a pacifying and non-threatening gesture. She stared at him a moment longer, uncertainty awash within her, yet, with a shudder, she took hold of his hand and allowed him to help her, though, at the contact she noticed once again how warm he was and the amazed thought spiraled through her mind like a wheel without a cart.

His amusement echoed in her ears. *"You think I should be cold as the dead?"* he asked derisively, receiving a bewildered glance in reply before she remembered how easily he could read her thoughts and she snatched her hand away from him, stepping back to speak out loud defiantly.

"How did you close the portal?"

He twisted to look at the glistening mirror, returning his hand to his face to shield his light-sensitive gaze. Turning his back on the portal, he stepped away from the glow, using his wings to protect him from the glare and Ayla could not help wondering why he had created such a profusion of light if it tormented him so greatly; then it was she who laughed dryly. Of course, it bothered him, he was a Dark One. Reviled. Cursed.

He spun back around to face her, his vast pinions arching toward her aggressively and his aura stretching out in the bright room, creating a shadow in spite of the radiance around him. "*Cursed?*" The thought filled her mind, the anger and resentment, which the word conveyed, making her cringe with dread. "*You call me cursed and reviled, but when I was taken as a child, who came to help me?*" His words pierced her like a jagged blade, but she could not respond in any manner as the emotions that accompanied his accusation crashed over her like a raging flood, forcing her to stumble backward unsteadily. Her shaking hands reached out, seeking stability, finding the back of an antique chair, which she strategically placed between them before she looked back up at him.

He was dangerous, indeed, and not simply because he was Dark. The powerful emotion he forced upon her was more than she could abide; nonetheless, he gave her no respite. Turning away from the Light, he flexed his dragonhide wings angrily, shadows twisting around him like a visual representation of his ire, in spite of the glimmer from the mirror. "*How self-righteous you of the Light are; is it any wonder none have come to seek help before?*" His thoughts filled her mind with waves of rage, abhorrence, and desolation. Although she raised her hands in a futile attempt to protect herself, her defense came to no avail. Staring down at her remorselessly, he could plainly see how she struggled to oppose the emotion he barely restrained. Smiling spitefully, he closed his eyes and opened himself to her completely, stretching out his arms as well as his broad wings to reveal the consuming, relentless, inundating fury and despair within him.

Ayla gasped in horror as the unanticipated deluge flooded over her with the power of a raging torrent. Stumbling in dismay, she fell backwards and knocked her head against the floor, the unabated surge of misery and rage washing over her and causing her to cry out in anguish. Raising her hands to cover her face, she shook her head violently, struggling to protect herself from the onslaught as she repeatedly cried out for him to stop, but she could read him all too easily.

Anger controlled him.

He had little concern for her comfort or security. He *wanted* to hurt her, to force her to experience the desolation that had been cast upon him. He did not relent. He *would* not relent. His crimson eyes were closed to her and all that existed was his torment, but the seemingly endless rush of agony was far more than she could physically bear.

Her heart-wrenching shriek of terror and pain shattered the brutality of his assault. Opening his eyes, he gazed down upon her as she writhed on the floor, wailing in unassailable grief. He watched her for a prolonged moment, transfixed by the sound of her weeping. It sounded so very familiar to him; as though she verbalized the suffering of his own heart and he could not tear his gaze away, but he did withdraw the cascade of emotion he had forced onto her. Stepping closer hesitantly, he felt an unfamiliar sensation tug at him, a sensation he little comprehended, but could not ignore.

Crouching down beside her, he laid his hand upon her trembling shoulder, attempting to distract her from her wailing; to rouse her from the trance cast over her by the lashing emotion he had hurled upon her so ruthlessly, but the contact of his hand brought forth another scream of such horror that he withdrew in dismay. Staring down at her unsure of how to proceed, he looked briefly at the light streaming from the mirror, contemplating his course while she continued to cry and thrash upon the floor in bitter lamentation.

Straightening, he glanced down at her briefly; then moved with a purposeful step toward the mirror, raising his hands as he drew nearer to shield his gaze from the brilliance streaming from the cracked glass. The radiance of light poured over him and he pressed his hands over his eyes with a groan of pain, protecting his sight from the piercing glow, but he could not shield himself otherwise from the seeking blaze. The light washed over him, around him, into him, its luminous intensity burning him like the sun on a summer day and the longer he stood, wings open, face up, unshielded except for his hands covering his eyes, the greater his pain became.

It started merely as discomfort, the light searing him like heat from a flame, but the sensation soon became much more intense, like being stung by unnumbered wasps, over and over and over. He hissed at the pain angrily, but he did not move away from the mirror and he did not wrap his wings round himself to block the burning glow. He stood unmoving, waiting, listening. Ayla was still weeping; the sound was as clear in his ears as the thudding of his heart in response to the light torturing him. The sting of the light melded with another, far more distressing feeling; a burning that spread over his entire body as if he were physically engulfed in flame and, in spite of his strength and determination, he could not suppress the cry of pain that forced its way past his bared teeth.

The sound brought Ayla back to her senses, but not only the sound; there was more than just the unexpected scream of a malefey, there was intense, burning, searing pain. Her eyes shot open as she gasped out loud, her gaze seeking the source of this new torment and what she saw made her stare in disbelief. *He stood before the mirror, bathed in its incandescent light, his flesh scorched and steaming, his hands clamped over his face, his wings arched backward in an unmistakable indication of suffering, yet he did not move.*

He screamed again and this time Ayla could see that she was not simply hearing the sound in her mind, reading his thoughts and hearing his voice inside her; he was screaming out loud. The sound and the sensation of burning she felt all over her body brought her to her feet in an instant and she rushed toward him, grasped him by his arm and tugged him away from the face of the mirror. Strong though he was, he did not resist her help; staggering backward, he retreated from the excruciating touch of the light as far as he was able to go until he pressed himself up against the far wall, his hands still covering his face, his mouth open as he gasped for breath, his fearsome wings pitched downward in exhaustion.

Ayla stared at him in utter confusion, then turned back to gaze at the mirror once again. The light was physically harmful to him; why had he done such a thing? She did not understand, yet even in his present state his answer came swiftly, though softly, breathlessly, and the sound did not emanate from his mind, but from his mouth. "You felt my pain. All of my pain. It was the only way to reach you."

Ayla stared at him in absolute horror, uncertain as to his entire meaning, but at that precise moment her comprehension was not nearly as important as protecting him from the light still streaming from the mirror, still washing over him causing him to gasp for breath and groan in pain. Turning her back, she looked round the room hastily, seeking anything she could use to protect him and, by protecting him, she would also reduce the pain she felt, since, as long as he stood in the light and suffered under its scorching contact, his continued torment was her own. As breathless as he, she desperately sought release of any kind, but there was nothing in the room she could use to cover the mirror and no way to block its sustained radiance.

Turning round again to gaze at him, the sight that met her eyes made her cry out in dismay. Unable to stand under the continual onslaught of light, he had slumped down against the wall to crouch upon the floor with his arms crossed over his head and his wings wrapped round about him as he shook fiercely. She stared for a moment, transfixed, fully aware of the deadly effect the searing light would have if he remained under its lethal blaze, but she did not stare long. Dashing toward him, she crouched down to touch his vast and ferocious wings, speaking as clearly as her own pain and astonishment at what she was doing would allow. "Come with me. I cannot cover the light, but the rest of the house is dark. Come with me!" Her urgent tone and the touch of her hands made him stop moaning. He uncovered his head to peer at her through splayed fingers still shielding his eyes.

"You must get out of the light," she said simply, getting up from her crouched position and pulling on one of the twelve inch spines of his wings; no longer terrified of their barbed cruelty or hideousness.

Even if she did not have the gift of empathetic sight, she would have known what she asked of him was far greater than he was capable of accomplishing alone. His skin was searing hot to the touch, his breathing was labored and uneven, and, in spite of everything she had ever been told about The Reviled, about their brutality, their malice, their impudence, when he uncovered his face and reached to take her hand she could see clearly that he was crying.

She would have stood and stared at the incongruous sight for untold measures, but his desperate state, of which she was fully aware, compelled her into further intercessory action. His strength had been stolen from him by the agonizing pain the light inflicted and he could barely unfurl his wings and hold them erect so that he might crawl behind her, but such a slow pace would not serve any useful purpose. Tugging on him, she urged him more imperatively; still, she could feel his weakness as it spread through his body and she knew his time was running out.

Standing beside him, she lowered herself to protect him from the light with her own body, shielding him by laying herself over him and moving with him as he struggled toward the door. Yet, even further than this, she laid her hands upon him, opening herself willingly to accept the full scope of his pain so that his vigor might return long enough for them both to escape the intensity of the deadly light. When she did, her cry pierced the room and he stopped to look upward at her.

Confused by the sudden rush of energy that returned to him, he did not contemplate the explanation for its return overlong; he knew the reason, it was clearer to him than anything else he had ever experienced. She had taken on his suffering, body and soul, transferring her strength to him in return for his weakness and her sacrifice caused more tears to sting his eyes and run over his cheeks. Clamoring up from his crawling position, he wrapped one arm about her even as she stumbled, even as she cried out in unrelenting pain, but it was momentary. Summoning every ounce of his remaining strength, he dragged her from the room, stepping out of the streaming luminosity of the mirror in the cool, sweet darkness of the hallway.

Released at last from the torment he had freely submitted to, he breathed a prodigious sigh and paused from pulling her along the dark corridor long enough to look round him uncertainly. He wanted to be as far from the light as possible, from any light, but he knew as well that darkness beckoned those of his tribe and that was a peril far more dangerous than the mirror's light. Although his sight was dimmed from the prolonged exposure to the mirror, his eyes adjusted swiftly to the dimness around them, like a feline able to see in virtual blackness he could see through the darkness that filled the small house and knew the parlor stood without illumination of any kind.

It was a risk worth taking.

Panting with exhaustion, he moved toward the darkness, half carrying Ayla, half dragging her as his strength was not much greater than her own. She stumbled along beside him, crying, though no longer screaming in pain, and for that he found he was inexplicably thankful. When the light of the mirror could no longer reach him in any fashion and he was, once again, cloaked in cool, soothing shadow, he stopped, lowered her carefully to the floor and stood over her; his head tilted upward, his eyes closed and mouth open as he breathed in the darkness deeply. His mind spun with echoes of writhing pain; his flesh burned with the memory of flame; his heart hammered in his chest and his entire body trembled with uncontrollable fatigue, but he did not move.

Gazing up at him in the darkness, Ayla considered him carefully, amazed beyond description. He stood over her, but did not threaten or intimidate her; he merely stood, almost vigilantly. Was he protecting her in the darkness? She looked more closely at him, now that he was no longer bathed in searing light nor submersed in shadows he had drawn to himself and she was amazed that she did not see the Dark One she had seen when she first looked upon him, when her fear had given her eyes the freedom of creating a demon. In fact, as he stood over her, breathing unsteadily, visibly trembling and with the water of tears still wet upon his face, she realized she had woefully misjudged him.

Reaching up with a trembling hand, she touched his fingers lightly, uncertain how he would react now that he was back in his native darkness, yet beginning to understand that she could trust him, in spite of his being one of the Reviled. The thought made her instantly shake her head. He was not at all like any tale she had ever been told about the Dark Ones, but she did not know what else to call him either, for she had never heard of a Dark Fey doing what he had done.

The timid contact of her hand made him open his eyes and look down upon her with an unreadable expression, yet before she could speak he stepped over her and moved away, directing his gaze out of the window in search of something. His Legion? The thought made her shudder instinctively, regardless of the tenuous thread of trust stretched taut between them, but it also made him turn his head and stare at her with an expression of such disapproval that no words were required. Recovered from her ordeal, she gathered her courage and spoke. "Why did you do that?"

He peered out the window silently and did not answer.

"You could have been killed," she reiterated, the concern in her voice making him turn back to stare at her in confusion, unfamiliar with the emotion she was conveying and uncertain how to respond to it.

"I may yet be killed." The deep tone of his reply made her shiver. Nothing he said made any sense to her, but before she could pose another question he laughed and shook his head. "Do you think the Light is the only danger I face tonight?"

She turned her head to the side. "I am no threat to you," she answered with bewilderment; her short-sightedness visibly annoying him. Satisfied that there were no shadows lurking in the darkness of the garden, he turned back to face her, impatience as evident in his expression as it was in the tone of his voice, the hue of his dark aura, and the feeling she sensed from him.

"No, Ayla, you were never a threat to me, but do you think those who were waiting for me to open the portal so they could cross and take from you everything they desired are now pleased with what I have done?" The question made her start violently; she had not considered that there were others of his kind who were waiting for him to invite them to partake in her ruin? Her instantaneous fear only served to agitate him further; nevertheless, he took no action against her, but rather closed his eyes and flexed his vast wings in a powerful display of constrained vexation.

"Then why did you do it?" she sighed sharply, becoming exasperated with his riddles; her minute show of anger making him smile. He moved closer to her with a measured pace.

"I have lived too many years under the torment of the Dlalth and you, Ayla, are the only one who can help me."

She stared at him blankly for a moment, entirely perplexed. "Help you?"

He smiled wryly and nodded, reading the questions tumbling through her mind and responding before she could articulate them. "Yes, Ayla," he affirmed her doubts as if speaking to a very small child, "you are the only one who is capable of discerning my true intentions."

She shook her head.

"You are The Guardian. You have the gift of Sight," he continued, his tone already belying his irritation at having to spell everything out for her. "You know what I am saying is truth or lies, do you not?" The edge of exasperation increased in his tone yet again, causing Ayla to shake her head, but retort with irritation of her own.

"Yes, of course, but how can I help *you*?"

He sighed sharply, moving closer to her to look down at her with a menacing glower and answering her with an edge to his tone that clearly indicated she ought to already know the answer to her question without having to ask him. "You can perform The Prevailation."

She shrank back from his antagonism, but shook her head, repeating the word with little understanding of what he meant, which brought a muffled growl to his lips. Turning away from her brusquely, he stalked towards the empty hearth, leaning upon the mantelpiece with one hand while he sought to restrain the anger swelling within him, but this further indication of his vexation only served to intimidate her all the more. The fragile thread of trust snapped.

"I do not know what you mean by Prevailation. I have never heard of such an act," she explained with tremulous fear shaking her voice. He shook his head. He was not surprised by her lack of knowledge with a rite that could assist a Dark One.

"Never taught the only ritual that can aid one who has been stolen from the light and forced into darkness," he muttered, palpably annoyed.

"You are one of the Reviled," Ayla attempted to restate her confusion, but he spun back to face her with an expression of such hatred and rage that she gasped, crossing her arms in front of her and stepping back from him so he could not strike her.

"I am NOT one of the Reviled!" he snarled. Infuriated, he stalked toward her once again with a measured pace; each step purposeful and unhurried; each step darkening his ethereal aura; each step bringing him closer to her in spite of the fact that she moved backward several times in sheer terror; each word he spoke deliberate and intractable. "I am a Fey of the Light, stolen from my home at the innocent age of seven and *forced* to endure The Integration! I will not, I *cann*ot describe to you the *immeasurable* anguish and torment I suffered *for years* at the hands of the Dlalth; a torment born by all young Fey who are taken and assimilated. But this misery was nothing, NOTHING, compared to the desolation of waiting for someone, anyone, to rescue me..." he paused, drawing a deep, unsteady breath, his powerful emotions inundating them both. "Someone to end my suffering and return me to my family and to the light... but no one EVER came."

Ayla could not suppress the wail of horror that escaped her as his despair engulfed her another time any more than she could prevent more tears from descending now that she understood the reason for his pain, but he was tired of her weakness and emotional displays. Moving closer still, he stopped only when he stood mere inches from her, leaning closer to speak into her face with such hostility that she could scarce draw breath. "You are the only person who can help me, Ayla, because you are the only one who can know with absolute certainty what I say is the truth; that I am not deceiving you to serve my own *evil* purposes."

Gasping in fear, she shook her head, but he would not accept her refusal.

"It is your gift, Ayla, and your purpose."

She stared at him silently as tears slipped over her flushed cheeks, utterly overwhelmed by him.

"Read me, Ayla!" he growled impatiently, but she reached up and shoved him away from her with as much force as she could manage.

"I cannot!"

His eyes narrowed suspiciously, "you *will* not."

"You are overpowering me!" she snapped back acerbically, "I cannot read through all that emotion."

He fell silent, considering, but he did not move away and he did not release her from the intense stare he had fixed upon her that pierced into her very essence and made her shudder. After a prolonged moment, he closed his eyes and slowly drew a deep breath; visibly calming himself before he stepped closer and reaffixed her with his resolute gaze. She watched him hesitantly, released from the waves of despondency and resentment he had again opened to her, yet still fearful of what he might do next.

Unhurriedly, he reached out for her hand, patient in a way he had not been before. She started away from him to search his eyes nervously for any indication of reassurance she might find there before offering her small hand to him. Holding it lightly in his warm clasp, he reached out for the other hand, waiting just as patiently for her to understand that he would do nothing atrocious should she give it to him as well. When she did, he drew both to himself, laying her hands upon his chest, palms down over his heart, before releasing his grasp upon her. Spreading his wings wide then, he turned his face upward, closed his eyes, and opened himself to her fully.

Ayla gasped in surprised revelation. She had never done such a thing before; never physically touched someone to read them while they stood, silently surrendered to her, revealing themselves in a manner that was intensely stirring and intimate; not even with Mardan had she shared such an unreserved moment.

The Dark One sighed sharply, redirecting her thoughts without speaking a word and she did not oppose him. Closing her eyes as well, she stretched out her senses, seeking the truth, avoiding the darkness and dejectedness that he held sequestered, sharing his thoughts and, after many protracted moments, his memories. Then, when she could see him in the clear light of sincerity, she could not contain the tears that slipped past her closed eyes as she touched the very essence of him; she could not withhold the moan that escaped her mouth at feeling his wretchedness, and she could not tear herself away from the inescapable desire to console him that suddenly filled her entire being.

Chapter Eight

"I do not want your sympathy Ayla," the Dark One said with his eyes still closed, as he stood unmoving; "I want your help."

Touching him body and soul, she finally understood what he was asking of her and the realization made her withdraw and step away from him. Opening her eyes, she stared at him as he stood motionless, his face still turned upward toward the ceiling, his vast wings still unfolded, his hands stretched out palms up.

"You want me to bring you back to the Light." She spoke the words breathlessly, terrified of everything his request represented. He nodded, but did not otherwise move.

What would become of her should she assist him? What would the Elders think? What would Mardan do? How could she explain to him why she would even consider such a dangerous undertaking? She laughed softly. She already had much to explain to him; actions she had taken that she could barely explain to herself. Hazards she had freely faced with no evidence that in doing so she would remain unharmed and she knew he would never understand why she continued to allow one of the Reviled to come so close to her, let alone to do the things he had done this night.

The Dark One opened his eyes with a formidable glare, lowering his wings with such force of action that the wind it created buffeted against her and shook her from her musings. Refocusing her attention, she reminded herself that he could read her every thought and she could not drift off to contemplate her relationship with a Celebrant while *he* was with her, yet even as she corrected her thinking, the Dark One sighed sharply and turned away. Cognizant that he was aware of her contemplations, she apologized without preamble. "You cannot expect me to simply forget about him."

"He is nothing. You are not concentrating on what is important, Ayla. We have little time!"

She stared back at him helplessly. "I do not know this ritual, The Prevailation; how can I perform it if I do not know it?"

He closed his eyes and shook his head subtly, a dry laugh escaping him in expression of his frustration with her. "I will teach you," he explained in a tone of exasperation, "I have learned it completely."

"But you are a Dark One, how," she began in astonishment, but he interrupted her with open hostility, cutting short her query.

"I am *not* a Dark One!"

Cringing, she raised her hands in a consolatory gesture. "I am sorry, but I do not know what else to call you."

"I have a name," he shot back petulantly, receiving a stare of surprise in response that made him laugh at her openly. Without a word, she waited for him to enlighten her, honestly curious, yet before he spoke again he moved to the window another time to inspect the dark woods for shadows. Rain had begun pouring down in torrents again and he knew the drumming sound it created would muffle any sound of approach. Long he stared out into the night, uncertain of what he saw. Shadows rippled in the deluge, images blurred. Shaking his head, he moved to the door and opened it silently, stepping out under the small portico to gaze more intently into the dark woods and what he thought he saw made his wings arch defensively. His stance became more aggressive and his aura contracted into a crimson shadow, but only briefly.

Shaking his head, he visibly relaxed. Satisfied that he saw none of his Legion, he stepped backward and closed the door, but Ayla did not distract him, uncertain if he was being watchful or if he did not wish to share his name; yet he turned back after many long moments and answered her as if as an afterthought.

"I am Gairynzvl," he said briskly, but the name was unfamiliar to her ear and she shook her head.

"Gair?" she asked apologetically.

"Gair *Runz* Vull," he repeated more phonetically, accenting and trilling the "R" rapidly. All malefey had names containing a trilled "R", just as all shefey held names containing a "Y." It was a tradition in the village of Hwyndarin. Fascination flickered across her delicate features at his unusual name. Yet, although she wished to inquire what such an uncommon name meant, his ill-tempered clarification plainly indicated to her that it was not the time for such curiosity, so she smiled dimly and nodded.

"Will you help me, Ayla?" he asked, urgency marking each word. "I can teach you the ritual, but we must hurry. I have closed a portal on my Legion and they will not wait to find another to come after me."

She stared back at him, wholly uncertain. "They will come tonight?" She attempted to clarify his statement, but he only nodded. "Is it a difficult rite? Have we time?" Her queries finally appeared to please him and a subtle smile turned his lips as he moved closer to her.

"They are not the only ones who may come tonight; you know this." His suggestion that Mardan would come to check on her made her realize that he was still reading her thoughts and his intrusive behaviour made her frown.

"Stop doing that," she snapped suddenly, her agitation making him smile more.

"Doing what?" The devilish expression that swept over his features made her shiver, but she did not appreciate the manner in which he toyed with her.

"I am not reading you without your permission. You should not read me." Even as she said the words she realized how ridiculous they sounded and she could not keep herself from smiling at the absurdity of their conversation. He smiled even more amiably and inclined his head to her.

"I am not reading you, Ayla," he assured with a warm tone he had not used before, "but if I was he; I would certainly come to check on you on such a dark night as this."

Her stare melted through him, but he only grinned and turned away, suggesting they sit down in order that he might better relate to her the Rite of Prevailation. She agreed hesitantly, as yet uncertain of her course, but her curiosity needed to be satiated and, if she could help him escape the torment of The Reviled, which she now understood far more thoroughly than she might have wished to, she was willing to try. As he began speaking, her mind filled with images of her youth; memories of sitting at an Elder's feet listening eagerly, chanting endlessly, and filling her mind with knowledge and magic. It had been difficult, yet immensely gratifying to learn the skills that would set her life to certainty and this present opportunity was no less intriguing, in spite of the danger involved.

Gairynzvl explained to her in greater detail how The Reviled hunted for criblings who were left untended or toddlefey left unguarded, stealing them away because they could not reproduce in the typical manner. These children, once taken, were subjected to cruelty and neglect, harrowed and haunted for years, which effectively turned them from the Light, creating monsters of callousness and malice, sociopathic and psychopathic alike. His descriptions brought tears to her eyes, but she forced them away, fully aware that there was little time, at present, to mourn for the unfortunate little souls.

He had been one such child, taken at an unusually older age, which made his transformation that much more difficult, both to endure and to achieve, yet, although the Dlalth were pitiless in their treatment of him, he never quite submitted. Ever rebellious, he had learned to separate himself from the despicable acts in which he was forced to participate and secretly began studying the ancient texts for any means of hope; any chance of escape he could find. He did not deny the torture was acute and there were many, many times he had done things he would forever regret, but this was all part of The Integration, designed specifically to break the spirit and instill anger, hatred and viciousness. Neither did he deny that he had copious amounts of each of those emotions within him, built up over years of anguish, but when he discovered the Rite of Prevailation, hope had been kindled within him that could not be extinguished.

Long into the night, he described the ceremony and its specific incantations, taking great care to teach her how to properly articulate each intrinsic word, since one small error of pronunciation would alter the invocation and create an unforeseen result. He also took time to explain the purpose of the rite, which was multifaceted. The ritual was designed to subvert the influence the Reviled had over their victims, release the subjected Fey from any connection with the Dlalth and their vile atrocities, and restore them to a more natural state of existence in the Light.

Ayla listened as closely as her weary condition would allow, but after several hours, as the rain subsided and the breaking light of dawn began to illumine the eastern horizon, she could combat sleep not longer. Repeatedly, her eyes closed against her wishes and he had to pause and rouse her back into attentiveness; yet at last, she raised her hands and begged him to stop.

"Please, Gairynzvl, I have to sleep."

He closed his eyes and breathed deeply, frustrated, although fully aware of the weariness in his own body, which could not be denied any more than hers.

Nodding, he agreed to a short respite; assuring her that he would stand guard while she slept lest any of his Legion come in the remaining hours of darkness. The Reviled could not cross in daylight or walk under the sun; thus, he would not sleep until daytide spread across the sky, and, although Ayla wondered at his own ability to seek her out during the hours of the day, her fatigue made questioning him at that particular moment impossible.

"I will answer that question another time," he told her quietly as she turned on the settee and settled in more comfortably, fully trusting him in spite of his crimson aura, dragon hide wings and continual propensity of reading her thoughts without permission.

Gairynzvl turned away with a grin, retracing his steps to stand beside the small window and gaze out into the lingering darkness of the forest as Ayla's breathing became softer and more rhythmic. The drumming rain had stopped, leaving in its place the melodious patter of myriad drops of water slipping, sliding toward the forest floor. Closing his eyes briefly, he breathed deeply and listened, allowing the gentle sounds to soothe his weariness and the vivid memory of pain still haunting his body.

Daylight slowly transformed the eastern sky with a pallet of colour, painting dim grayish-greens across the edge of the world that faded into lavender hues and streaks of pink, orange and yellow as the bright disc of the sun returned to the sky from its nightly sojourn. When, at last, he felt safe under its potent light, he turned his back to the window and stepped toward the center of the room.

Ayla slept peacefully, her aura glowing softly luminescent with pink and golden tones that reflected her tranquility and he could not keep himself from watching her. Quietly, cautiously, he returned to the settee, standing behind it to gaze down on her thoughtfully. Had it been any other time, he would have had few options; his choices regarding her would have been determined by his Legion and her tranquility would have been shattered irrevocably. Yet now, in the cool light of early morning with the songs of larks and jays echoing through the brightening forest he was finally free to stand, unhindered, and look upon her beauty.

Her pale, roseleaf complexion glowed with the blossoms of youth, as did her flaxen hair that spilled about her shoulders like gossamer silk. Her features were delicate and beautiful and the curves of her lissome frame drew his gaze. Never before had he enjoyed the opportunity to look upon such a lovely Fey without the clamor of raucous obscenities and ruthless expectations being hurled at him. He had never before had a choice and the liberation made him dizzy.

Reaching to steady himself, he laid his hands upon the back of the settee as his wings spread wide for balance and he stared down at her, entirely captivated. A warm blush spread over her cheek and she smiled subtly, a quiet sigh escaping her, as if, even in sleep, she remained aware of his emotions. The pleasure she experienced spread through her aura, causing the hues to shift to deeper, rosier tones and Gairynzvl had to fight back the reckless temptation to touch her.

The last thing he wanted to do was frighten her again!

Forcing himself to look away from her, he struggled against the sudden pounding that spread within him and stared upward at the ceiling while breathing in deeply, amazed at the honest rush of sensation hammering through him.

And in that moment, everything changed.

A thunderous crash broke the silence filling the room and light flooded inward. Ayla screamed, even before waking fully, and curled into a protective ball upon the settee as the sound of voices echoed about her, harsh words clashing like swords. At the first sound, Gairynzvl spun about to face the unexpected danger. Pushing back his broad wings, he sheltered her from view as much as he was able, fearing his Legion had located him and forced their way through the brightening morning to deliver retribution, but as he turned, a powerful blow crossed his face and he stumbled backward.

Tumbling to the floor, Ayla scrambled away from the fray, seeking safety in spite of not clearly understanding what was happening. When she reached the far side of the room where she could cower behind a tall wooden book cabinet, she peered past its shielding structure and watched, horrified, as her Celebrant friend and lover flexed his broad, brilliantly white wings, turned deftly and delivered a brutal kick that caught Gairynzvl across the shoulder, cheek and chin that sent him stumbling, but his crimson, dragon hide wings countered his balance before he could fall. Stretching outward, he slashed with a twelve-inch spine like a blade and a bright crimson gash opened across Mardan's chest.

"Vile, ruthless demon," he cursed loudly, gasping at the pain searing across his chest while his opponent regained his balance and momentum. "Come again, cursed ghoul!" Re-centering himself, Mardan faced him more squarely, offering his fists as a focus, but when Gairynzvl stepped closer, Mardan spun and dropped, sweeping his rivals feet from under him and watching with a vitriolic sneer as he fell backward onto a small glass table that smashed into daggers, which ripped and gashed at him ruthlessly.

Ayla screeched in horror and stepped out from behind the cabinet, unable to watch the conflict and not attempt to intercede, but, although Gairynzvl turned his head to look at her, concern clearly expressed in his crimson eyes as well as through the unmistakable emotion of protectiveness he directed to her in unspoken thought, Mardan neither looked at her nor paused in his attack. Stepping forward with a purposeful stride, he stared down at the Dark Fey lying at his feet and spoke a single, intractable word.

"Cruciavaeryn!"

At hearing the word, Gairynzvl screamed loudly and cringed into a knot as waves of unrelenting, excruciating agony pierced his body, again and again and again. His cries of torment did not compel Mardan to break the Spell of Inflicted Pain he had cast. Moving to stand over the Reviled One, he looked down unsympathetically and watched him writhe as he considered his options. Even as he did so; even as Gairynzvl thrashed and screamed, Ayla straightened quietly. Her amber eyes wide with horror. Was this the Fey who had claimed her heart for so long? Was this her Celebrant friend and lover? How could he possibly be so remorselessly cruel? She watched him observing his fallen, suffering foe and shook her head slowly, anger and revulsion permeating her entire being.

Squaring her shoulders defiantly, she did not speak a single word. She did not cry out pleadingly. She did not attempt to force him to stop what he was doing in any manner; rather, she drew a deep, shuddering breath and closed her eyes. Stretching out her shaking hands, her delicate wings, and her exceptional senses, she psychically touched Gairynzvl and accepted his pain.

Her shriek of agony pierced the small room the moment her senses reached him and torrents of pain unlike anything she had ever experienced flooded over her unrelentingly. The pain was far greater than the torment of light from the mirror, which they had both borne only a few short hours earlier. Arching in excruciating distress, Ayla's cry only ceased when she could no longer breathe, but even then she stared blindly at the ceiling, open mouthed and paralyzed by the waves of agony rushing over her.

Mardan turned abruptly, recalling her extraordinary gift far too late and staring in horror at her, instantly regretting his decision to use a spell of such brutality; yet even while his attention was momentarily redirected, Gairynzvl opened his eyes to glare up at him with absolute hatred. Freed from the greater portion of the spell's vicious torment by Ayla's selfless act, he drew a deep, ragged breath, gathered his strength beneath him like a tiger preparing to spring, and pushed up off the floor. The solitary beat of his powerful wings created such momentum of force that he physically knocked Mardan from his feet and pinned him to the floor in a single motion.

Ayla gasped loudly and crumbled beside them, convulsing violently. Turning to stare at her with tears of pain still visible in his crimson eyes, Gairynzvl pressed a barbed spine upward into the soft skin beneath Mardan's chin, fully aware of the precise pressure required to cause the greatest measure of pain without drawing blood. Then he spoke, his deep voice a growl that was not to be ignored.

"Retract your vile spell before you kill her!"

Mardan did not argue; closing his eyes briefly to center his thoughts. "Dlynn-zalus," he said in as equally a commanding tone as he had utilized to impose the spell. Instantly the pain subsided and passed away.

The release was euphoric and, although Gairynzvl could not help closing his eyes and breathing a deep sigh with profound relief when the stabbing, burning, caustic pain left his body, he did not withdraw the twelve-inch barb from his foe's throat and Mardan did not oppose him. Both turned their heads to look at Ayla with immense concern as her convulsing diminished, but it did not stop as anticipated. Her eyes were open and her glazed, unfocused stare betrayed the gravity of her situation. She had willingly taken unto herself a torment that was a vast deal greater than she had strength to bear.

Gairynzvl looked back at Mardan and pressed the spine of his wing even deeper into the soft flesh under his chin, speaking with a tone more urgent than before. "Release her, you monster!"

Mardan subtly shook his head. "I have withdrawn the spell, but it was designated for you, not her." His explanation did not satisfy and Gairynzvl shook his head, flexing his broad wings as he righted himself from his kneeling position over his opponent to move closer to her instead.

"Designated for me," he repeated uncomprehendingly as he crouched down beside her and watched her anxiously. Mardan grasped his throat in an attempt to alleviate the lingering pain he felt, but clambered to his feet, as well, and stepped cautiously closer while more thoroughly clarifying his statement.

"You are malefey; she is shefey. I spoke the spell upon you and created it to be potent enough to subdue your greater strength and endurance." Gairynzvl stared up at him vengefully, his thoughts filling with the desire for retribution, but his immediate concern was Ayla who still gasped and shook fiercely.

"I was not thinking," Mardan admitted with evident regret. "I did not think she would do such a thing for one of the Reviled." His tone of contempt pushed Gairynzvl beyond his limits and he sprang back to his feet and moved to within inches of his rival, staring remorselessly into his cerulean eyes while he spoke with taut restraint.

"She would do *such a thing* for anyone and if you knew her *at all* such actions on her part would not surprise you."

Mardan's gaze narrowed angrily at his indictment, but Gairynzvl continued before he could formulate a rebuttal.

"Your ignorance may cost her her life. What do you intend to do, *Celebrant?*"

Mardan leaned closer to him threateningly, but did not follow through on his inclination to reach for his throat; rather, he stepped round the Dark Fey before him to kneel down beside the Fey he loved. Touching her shoulder gently, he bowed his head and uttered a barely perceptible prayer; his actions turning Gairynzvl's stomach with their appearance of hypocrisy. Standing over them both, he watched with palpable anxiety. Unable to stand still and incapable of turning away, he did not know what to do. His entire life had been a lesson in ruthlessness, not concern or compassion. He had no knowledge of healing or prayers and had little patience to learn.

Mardan took hold of Ayla's convulsing body more securely, drawing her into an embrace that cradled her close to his chest as he wrapped his magnificent wings around her, bowed his head and began speaking a soft incantation. Gairynzvl watched for a moment, then turned away, the sight of his foe holding her so closely, so tenderly, creating a sensation within him he could neither comprehend nor disregard. With agitation twisting inside him like a pit of vipers, he returned to the window and gazed outward with an intense stare. He tried to refocus on the potential threat of his Legion, but, although he tried, he could not distract himself.

Turning back, he watched from the window as Mardan continued to speak the incantation. The words were spoken in the High Language of Celebrae and were unfamiliar to him, but even from the window he could feel a stirring within his heart he had never felt before, a lifting sensation, a release of some kind. It drew him back to the pair on the floor like a moth to a flame. Incapable of closing himself off from the inherent magic of the invocation, Gairynzvl stood over them once again, gazing down with a potent combination of vexation, confusion and a sensation of optimism entirely foreign to him.

Ayla gasped suddenly for breath, deep and long, as if she had stopped breathing altogether. She shuddered spasmodically, then relaxed. Uncertain if her behavior was promising or cause for even greater concern, Gairynzvl could not contain his queries of apprehension, but Mardan ignored him. Rising from his kneeling position, he lifted her in his arms and carried her to the settee where he laid her down gently, straightened, and breathed a deep sigh.

"I have done all I am able to do. She must do the rest." Mardan spoke quietly, turning to gaze with restrained ire upon the Dark One who stood watching with the most perplexing expression of worry upon his pallid features.

"Why are you here with her? What are your intentions, *Dark One?*" he asked in an authoritative tone, years of training as a Celebrant, as well as a lifetime of ingrained distrust for The Reviled, revealing themselves in his every word and action. Gairynzvl responded in the only manner he knew. Stepping closer to him aggressively, he spat his response back at him petulantly.

"You do not truly wish to know why I am here, *Celebrant. Y*ou only want to find some reason to justify your behaviour."

"My behaviour requires no justification; if I had not intervened when I did," Mardan began defensively.

"I would have done nothing," Gairynzvl's tone betrayed his increasing ire and he stepped closer still, argumentatively.

"Nothing?" Mardan's reply was concise and acerbic, his disbelief apparent. Again, Gairynzvl moved forward, his every action inciting disagreement; each motion generating conflict.

"You are so sure of yourself. So convinced you are right in everything you do that you cannot see how evil you are inside." Quicksilver, Mardan reached forward, struggling not to obey his desire to choke the life from the irksome creature standing before him, flagrantly taunting him into actions that would be his own destruction. Grasping the Dark One by his coat, rather than his neck, Mardan leaned closer as well until they were, once again, only inches from each other; cerulean and crimson locked in a hateful glare.

"If Ayla were not here," he began, but Gairynzvl finished his sentence, reading his thoughts as easily as he had read hers.

"You would speak a curse far more dire than the last one and leave me to suffer in endless agony?" Mardan stared at him, amazement flooding over his features at hearing his own thoughts verbalized by another. "And you call *me* Dark One."

"Stop."

The softly spoken word broke through their ceaseless quarreling and both turned to look down upon Ayla with surprise. She had opened her eyes and was watching them wearily, tears sliding over her pale cheeks, which had just a short while ago been rosy with the blossoms of youth. Now she appeared visibly older, as if, in bearing the Spell of Inflicted Pain meant for one of The Reviled, she had taken on so great a burden it had actually stolen years from her life-force.

The bickering males glanced at each other with shared uneasiness, but it was Gairynzvl who stepped closer, while Mardan stood frozen; his thoughts still reeling as a result of what the Dark One had just said to him and the revelation of bitter truth it exposed. Crouching down beside the settee slowly, Gairynzvl looked into her tired gaze, laying his hand beside hers on the cushion as he spoke quietly to her through his thoughts, rather than through words that would be easily overheard by his adversary.

"*Do not trouble yourself, Ayla; I will not fight with your Celebrant again.*" His words rang clear in her mind and she closed her eyes, sensing his acceptance of her continued loyalty to Mardan, but she slowly shook her head. Unable to speak, she thought her reply. She felt it; sharing with him the startling discovery that she no longer loved Mardan. She could not after what she had witnessed in him and what she had felt from him. Her loyalty no longer centered upon him, but, rather, was growing each moment in strength and vitality for another; one who was dark, but far more compelling than Mardan could ever hope to be.

Gairynzvl stared at her in absolute amazement, never anticipating that she should reveal something so profound to him or that she should even feel that which would have, just a day ago, been unimaginable. Left without words, either spoken or thought, he sought to express himself in the only manner he was capable of and, in spite of the one who stood silently watching. Moving his hand slowly, he covered her chilled and still trembling fingers with his own, shook his head indistinctly, and smiled.

"Rest. I will not leave you alone," he whispered softly to her, fully aware that she was already slipping into an exhausted sleep. He watched her for a brief moment, then regained his feet and turned back to face Mardan, looking up at him menacingly from his downturned face.

"She does not want us to fight," he revealed in a low tone, exposing the truth of what his adversary had already guessed; that they were able to communicate in a non-verbal and far more intimate manner than he and Ayla had ever shared. His irritation at this discovery was conspicuous, but he stood his ground out of respect for her and did not retaliate. "She told you as much?"

Gairynzvl nodded unhurriedly, unable to deny himself the pleasure of tormenting his rival with the fact, which clearly annoyed him. Still, Mardan only nodded sharply and moved towards the door. Turning back then, he added disdainfully,

"I cannot convince myself that she should be safe in your keeping alone; therefore, I shall not continue to fight you, but neither shall I leave." Not waiting for a response, he turned then and stepped outside into the warm light of the morning sun, leaving the door wide so that the streaming luminescence poured into the room, anticipating that such an effect would be intolerable to the Dark One he left behind. Gairynzvl only laughed and turned into the brilliant glow, stretching out his wings to their fullest, turning his face into the warmth of the sun for the first time in his adult life to enjoy its full radiance upon him.

…until Mardan stepped away from the door.

Chapter Nine

Ayla slept through the remainder of the morning and most of the afternoon, stirring only slightly from the depths of absolute exhaustion. During these tense hours, the two malefey kept an uneasy vigil, one outside the small cottage, the other inside, and although they did not speak to each other, they repeatedly glared in the other's direction through either the open door or the parlor window. Their mutual dislike was far more than apparent and for more reasons than the simple fact that one was a Celebrant and the other a Dark One.

Satisfied that his Legion would not trespass into the daytide to deliver retribution for his act of defiance in closing, rather than opening, the portal of Ayla's mirror and cheating them out of their pitiless amusement, Gairynzvl sat down on the floor beside the settee where she slept and closed his eyes, weary beyond measure. He had kept a long watch during the previous evening waiting for darkness to fall while protecting her from his Legion by insisting on coming to confront her alone and open the portal. Then he had performed the difficult magic that closed the portal while struggling with her and blocking his thoughts back to the Legion so they would not immediately realize what he was doing.

Convincing her of his trustworthiness by bearing the full torment of the Light had been even more dangerous than defying his Legion, nearly fatal, but he had succeeded in persuading her. This act had achieved his purpose, yet it was even more useful in gaining her confidence than he initially intended. Still, the taxing hours of the night, which had culminated in a battle for his life not with his Legion, but with a Celebrant of the High Faith who was potentially even more dangerous than they were, in addition to standing guard over Ayla while she slept had taken an exacting toll. Nevertheless, he did not trust falling asleep in the presence of a Celebrant. It was entirely possible that, should he lose himself in slumber, he might awaken in bonds, or worse.

Attempting to rest without losing awareness of his surrounds, he listened intently for any suspicious sounds while allowing his thoughts to cease their fretful spinning and his body to relax. When he finally managed to quiet them, Ayla stirred, turning on the settee for the first time since the morning and reaching out in her sleep to place her small hand lightly upon his broad shoulder. He flinched at the unexpected contact, twisting to look at her curiously. Unsure if she had roused herself, he found that she remained asleep and he gazed with weary wonder at the delicate blush that warmed her pale cheeks.

Gairynzvl smiled curiously, inquisitive to discover how far her abilities extended while she slept. Reaching without turning around, he returned her light touch and smiled warmly, permitting his thoughts to drift in a romantic direction he had rarely, if ever, allowed them to wander and she sighed contentedly in response.

A promising reaction, but not very conclusive. He needed more.

Drawing a deep breath, he let his thoughts shift again. This time they were not pleasant. Instead, he recalled the harsh memories of callous atrocities he had been forced to undertake by his Legion and the ruthlessness with which he had been compelled to perform them. The revulsion and distress he had experienced as a result of these actions, both when he had been forced to take them and at that moment, were acute, but he took great pains not to share the full scope of his memories. The result of his experiment, however, was irrefutable.

Ayla gasped and pulled her hand back, her lashes fluttering as she moaned and tossed her head fitfully as she sought to escape the source of misery filling her mind, but he did not release her. Nodding with certainty that she could read him, and perhaps anyone, even in her unconscious state, he twisted about and reached with both hands to calm her dismay by once again filling his thoughts with peaceful images and soft, unspoken words that soothed her fear.

He had never taken pains to calm someone before. He had never been given the liberty to do anything so sympathetic, but seeing how she relaxed under the influence of his gentle touch and reassuring thoughts filled him with a sensation he could barely comprehend. Perhaps this strange emotion was a lingering effect from exposing himself to The Light of the mirror. Perhaps it was a natural result of spending so much time with Ayla, a Fey of the Light so different from any other that he could not tear himself from her presence. Whichever it was, he felt suddenly as if he were two distinctly different Fey: One Dark, One Light, each one twisting round the other, locked in a perpetual battle.

Staring at her intensely, his thoughts filled with new contemplations he had never guessed he would ever be free to ponder, but he did not watch her long before his eyes closed of their own volition. His weariness overwhelmed him; nevertheless, he struggled to get to his feet and crossed the parlor floor to stand at the end of the hallway looking toward the light streaming from the room with the mirror and the nursery beyond. He had nearly forgotten, but the childfey Ayla had been tending the night before, whom he had set under a sleeping spell, would soon be waking. Turning he looked back at her. She was still sleeping upon the settee and he wondered if he should waken her. He certainly could not care of the cribling himself.

Moving back towards the center of the parlor, he noticed Mardan standing just outside the door looking upward toward the canopy of the forest with his broad wings held tense as if he heard or had seen something that made him vigilant. Without reconsidering, Gairynzvl moved slowly to the door, His fatigue was evident and spoke with a notably lethargic tone. "Celebrant."

Mardan turned to glare at him, his expression clearly indicating his annoyance at being disturbed and he spoke in a markedly derogatory manner. "Dark One."

Gairynzvl closed his eyes in vexation, but was far too tired to argue. "There is a childfey," he said simply and Mardan's eyes grew wide in confusion.

"A childfey? Where?"

Gairynzvl flexed his wing to point towards the back room where the nursery was located as Mardan stepped beneath the eaves of the small portico and came inside. "Ayla was tending him last night," he began, intending to explain what had occurred during the hours of the night, but his suggestion that he had been with her since the evening before visibly incensed his Celebrant rival.

"Last night! Just how long have you been here, you vile Spined Fey?" His continued disparagement pushed Gairynzvl to his limits once again. Stepping menacingly closer, he retorted with ire, each word measured and intractable.

"Do not call me that again, *Celebrant*, unless you truly desire to know what damage my spines can do." Mardan matched his aggressive stance with one of his own, but Gairynzvl pointed once again down the hall. "The childfey. He will be waking soon and will need care."

Raising his brow in amazed skepticism, Mardan considered a moment and then glanced toward the nursery, noticing the radiant light streaming out into the hallway from one of the other rooms. "What have you done to him?" His implication only served to vex Gairynzvl even more. Spinning on his heel, Gairynzvl stalked away from him back towards the settee.

"For the love of the Ancients," he growled ferociously, "Would you rather I waken Ayla?"

Mardan stared at him, entirely perplexed by his behavior. Turning his head slightly to one side, he took a single step toward the hall, then queried further. "Why are you here, Dark One? What is it you want, if not the childfey and not Ayla?" Silence answered him; silence and a stare of such exasperation that he decided it best to forego pressing his inquiries and moved quietly down the hall toward the light spilling out into the otherwise darkened corridor. The light illuminated the closed door of the crib room.

In his absence, Gairynzvl returned to Ayla's side and gazed down at her with a glazed expression, his thoughts spinning with fatigue. A sudden and unexpected yearning spread through him that he was not entirely certain how to manage. More than anything else he wanted to lie down with her, enwrap her in his close embrace and sleep. There was no pounding, hammering desire; no wrenching hunger; no thoughts that spiraled downward in the chasm of lust, only a longing to hold her and to be held by her. A yearning to trust and be trusted and to rest without apprehension as he had not done since before The Reviled had stolen him away.

The ache inside him grew out of proportion, fueled by his exhaustion and a possibility he had never before allowed himself to dream. Unable to bear the sensation, he lowered himself to the floor where he had been resting previously, wrapped his wings round himself, and closed his eyes as irrepressible tears assaulted him. Covering his head with his arms, he fought their violent attack, but the devastating hope that had been kindled inside him made continued suppression of his misery all but impossible.

For too long he had been tormented by brutality and scathing derision, forced to hurt others or be hurt himself or both. For too long he had struggled to retain a shred of his former life and keep a flicker of Light aflame within his heart while desolation and agony threatened to overtake him every single day. Shaking fiercely, he tried to combat the torrents of emotion flooding over him, pouring out of him, but it was useless. He could not contain the deluge any more than he could withstand the light of the mirror and the unbearable cascade of pain and loneliness drowning him felt just as lethal.

Opening her eyes, Ayla looked round her woozily, her head spinning and body aching, but it was not this discomfort that had awakened her. Rather, it was a sense of overwhelming sorrow that had permeated her dreams. Even before opening her eyes, she knew the source of the bitter emotion, not because Gairynzvl was sitting right beside her on the floor or because she could hear him crying, but because she had already grown accustomed to his thoughts in her mind and the sound of his voice even when he was not physically speaking.

The pain was the same as it had been hours before when he had hurled his misery upon her so forcefully. It was so powerful she could barely contain it and so desolate she could hardly withstand it, but she reached out and touched him gently, taking care to think his name very clearly before laying her hand upon the crown of his head so the unexpected contact would not instantly alarm him. Even so, the tender touch of her hand made him shudder and she could hear and feel the intensity of his emotion increase.

"Please, do not cry," she said softly beside him, uncertain where Mardan had gotten to, but sure she did not want him to see or hear them. Gairynzvl shook his head, unable to speak. Sitting up, she positioned herself with her legs on either side of him so she could lean over him from behind and offered an embrace that entirely encircled him. Her openly affectionate hug made him shudder again and he reached backward without turning round to return her clasp as best he was able until the tide of poignant emotion finally ebbed. In the poignancy of the moment, neither was aware of Mardan when he returned from the nursery with Roshwyn.

Seeing them, he stopped suddenly, a rush of resentment and anger swelling within him, but he was not deaf to the sound of crying he had heard moments before and he was fully aware of the fact that the tears were not Ayla's. Standing statuesque with the babe in one arm, gently supported by a cradling wing, he watched them silently. He was uncertain what she saw in the Dark One that she found so compelling, but it soon became apparent that she sensed him. Looking up from their prolonged embrace, she gazed into Mardan's cerulean gaze with tear-filled eyes.

Disengaging herself from Gairynzvl's clinging, child-like embrace, Ayla moved across the room to where Mardan stood and offered to take the babe, but he shook his head, leaning closer to speak more confidentially. "What does he want from you Ayla? Why is he here? Why did he not simply take Roshwyn and go and what did he do to the mirror?" His questions were all valid, but Ayla shook her head.

"I must help him, Mardan."

Unsatisfied, he repeated himself. "But why? What does he want?"

She stammered, unsure if she should tell a Celebrant the true reason why one of The Reviled sat crying on her parlor floor, but when she twisted about to look back at him, she knew with certainty that she could not proceed without the help that only he, being a Celebrant, could provide. Gairynzvl had not finished telling her about The Prevailation, but having been well educated in ancient texts, spells and incantations, she could make logical assumptions.

"Have you ever heard of a rite called The Prevailation?" she asked hesitantly, watching with growing anxiety as Mardan's expressive features darkened with concern. He shook his head.

"You cannot Ayla." He attempted to dissuade her, but she looked back again at the Dark One still crying on her floor.

"How can I not? Look at him, Mardan."

He straightened to look over her cautiously, openly confused, yet unconvinced. "I see him, but are not the Reviled known also to be Deceivers? Is he leading you astray for his own purposes?" He raised justifiable questions, but Ayla shook her head. She knew only too well the honest misery the Dark One had suffered. The misery he still suffered.

"They are, yes, but you must believe me, I have felt his pain." As she spoke, Mardan's expression shifted to incredulity, one eyebrow rising skeptically. "You know my gifts, Mardan. You know how easy it is for me to discern truth from lies. I have been trained how to do it by the Elders themselves. I have known how to do it all my life."

Unwilling to believe that a Dark One might even understand what it meant to suffer; Mardan shook his head once again and drew a deep breath, trying desperately to understand her. "You have felt his pain?" he repeated doubtfully, unsure what she truly meant and not at all certain he really wished to know, but she nodded.

"Yes, Mardan, I have read him." She paused, drew a deep breath and continued, "he shared his pain with me."

Growing irritated, Mardan looked away from her, clenching his jaw in order not to say anything he might instantly regret. In his arms, Roshwyn fretfully shifted and cried unhappily, reaching for Ayla.

"He shared it with you?" he repeated, handing the wriggling child to her before turning his back and moving toward the door.

"I had to be certain he was telling the truth." She hurried after him, desperate to explain. "If I had not made certain, would you not, now, be even more angry?" Attempting to hush the fussing babe, she began a gentle rocking motion, but it was the tone of their increasingly discordant conversation that distressed the childfey and no amount of rocking, bouncing or aimless walking would soothe his wailing.

"I would be, yes, but Ayla, do you forget everything we have shared? How can you disregard my feelings? And yours?" Mardan turned back to capture her with a piercing gaze and she could not ignore the heartbreak and disappointment she sensed from him. Wincing, she shook her head, searching herself for greater sympathy for him after all they had shared, but could not otherwise answer. Roshwyn's crying became a full bawl. She shifted him in her arms to try to comfort him better, but could not calm him.

Even as they stood staring at each other with palpable disappointment, Gairynzvl got up from the floor and moved purposefully closer to them. Mardan stepped forward protectively, his only thought the childfey, but he stopped just as suddenly and stared, dumb-struck, when the Dark Fey gently took the nearly hysterical childling from Ayla's ineffectual embrace. Cradling him in his arms while folding his wings backward out of view, he stroked the babes rosy cheeks with a tenderness of affection that quieted the wee one almost instantly. Moving slowly, he stepped away from the quarreling pair without speaking. Turning his back on them, he walked into the late day sunlight streaming through the open back doorway and warmed the babe in their temperate rays while rocking him gently.

Ayla turned to look up at Mardan who watched the Dark One with disbelief and confusion, but he could no longer argue about his character. A childfey knows truth. They instinctively understood another's true intent and the simple fact that Roshwyn not only accepted the touch of one of the Reviled Fey but ceased his wailing and began to coo and gurgle contentedly in his embrace spoke volumes. Gazing down at Ayla, he nodded, but reached to draw her closer to speak more confidentially.

"Listen to me, Ay, you cannot perform The Prevailation. It is far too dangerous," he began insistently, but she interrupted him with a defiant tone shaking her head vehemently.

"If I can help him, I will not turn aside."

He smiled at her stubbornness and shook his head. "You cannot, not in your present state."

She attempted to argue further, but he raised his hands to forestall anything else she might attempt to say. "Hear me, Ayla! The Prevailation is extremely dangerous, not only for the one performing it, but also for the one receiving the rite." As he spoke, he glanced up at Gairynzvl who had turned to listen to their discussion without diverting his attention from the cribling in his arms. Assured that he was, in fact, listening, Mardan continued with a tone meant for both of them to hear. "I have never actually witnessed the ceremony, but I am familiar with it and I am fully aware of how much is at risk. After what you have just been through, Ayla, you simple do not have the strength."

Once again she attempted to argue, but Mardan moved past her, addressing his next words specifically at the Dark One who lifted his crimson gaze to stare at him with a potent combination of insolence and trepidation.

"If you are to escape the wrath of your Legion, The Prevailation must be performed right away, but even doing as much you will still be in jeopardy. You know this."

Gairynzvl nodded, but said nothing.

"Ayla is not capable of undertaking the rite, even if she had not just borne the spell of pain intended for you. She is simply not powerful enough."

Gairynzvl's eyes narrowed as he glared back at Mardan, but he was careful to temper his anger so he would not distress the babe falling asleep in his arms. "You would not permit her in any case," he began, yet before he could finish his thought Mardan shook his head and interjected resolutely.

"No, I would not. It is far too dangerous for her under any circumstance." He paused considering, his cerulean gaze locking with vexed crimson. "However," he turned and glanced back at Ayla before returning his gaze to the Dark One before him. "It is not too dangerous for me."

Crimson and cerulean locked and for a long moment neither said anything, but the skepticism clearly evident in Gairynzvl's expression brought further clarification from Mardan at last. Shaking his head, his wings lowered considerably as he spoke in a less authoritative tone. "I have treated you unfairly,

Dark One, and I willingly apologize. You are, apparently, far more than what you seem."

Ayla knew instantly that he spoke the truth, but Gairynzvl searched his expression cautiously before nodding subtly, never having received an apology from anyone before and not at all sure how to respond. After an awkward silence, he returned less confrontationally. "My name is Gairynzvl." He corrected him in a notably weary tone and looked down at the now sleeping babe in his arm. Mardan nodded, repeating the unusual name to lock it in his memory and watching with growing concern as the Dark One covered a yawn and closed his eyes.

"When have you slept last?"

Ayla stepped forward to take Roshwyn even as Gairynzvl wavered lethargically and shook his head. "I cannot tell you," he replied in a mutter. He had been on his guard for days, preparing for the moment when he would cross and confront Ayla, close the portal, and attempt to convince her of his true intentions, but he had been unprepared for the strength that endeavor had required. He had been even less ready to face a Celebrant in a fight that might have claimed his life had it not been for Ayla's intervention. He was exhausted and could not hide the fact. Mardan shook his head.

"You must regain your strength. The Rite of Prevailation is prolonged and taxing and not at all to be undertaken in a weakened condition."

"But we must perform it before night falls," Ayla insisted anxiously, rocking the childfey gently in her arms as he settled. Gairynzvl nodded, yet barely heard either of them, so great was his fatigue. Taking control of the situation, Mardan stepped closer and held the Dark One with a steadying grasp, leading him to the settee so he could sit down as he set out their plan.

* * *

While Gairynzvl slept under Mardan's vigilant guardianship to regain some of his strength, Ayla traveled with all due haste to her friend Nayina's home where she made a brief explanation that she needed her assistance in watching Roshwyn for the night. Her friend was only too pleased to undertake his care, having no childfey of her own at present and supposing Ayla's request came as a result of an unplanned evening to be spent with Mardan. Unaware of how equally correct and incorrect she was, she did not argue when Ayla swiftly bid her good eventide, nor did she make any attempt to prolong her visit with casual conversation, but stood quietly watching her as she departed, a mischievous glimmer in her eyes.

As she returned to her cottage, set on the outskirts of the village, Ayla searched the forest around her apprehensively, certain at any moment a gruesome Reviled Legionnaire would break from the cover of the closing dusk to chase after her, but the evening was lazy and quiet with only the soft chirruping of crickets and the monotone whirring of cicadas breaking the stillness. A cool breeze of twilight had begun to twist and dance among the leafy canopy overhead, and the monarchs of the forest tossed their heads and sighed; shaking countless fireflies from their beds, which scattered like starlight in the gathering shadows.

Yet in all of this calm tranquility, Ayla sensed a growing threat. Rank and indolent even at the distance it was, she could not mistake it for anything other than what it was and the realization of its approaching presence spurred her to her greatest speed.

The Legion was coming.

Chapter Ten

Mardan listened to Ayla's account upon her return from Nayina's house and shook his head. "If the Legion is coming, we cannot perform the Prevailation." His pronouncement brought a glare to Gairynzvl's eyes, but he said nothing. "We do not have time. The Rite can take hours. You know this," Mardan added insistently. Gairynzvl's glare intensified and he got up from the settee where he had awakened only moments earlier and stepped closer to the fair Fey ominously. His tone was sharp with accusation.

"We would have had time if it had not been for *your curse.*"

Ayla felt the rising agitation between them and cringed when Mardan rebuked him just as caustically. "*My* curse has nothing to do with this."

"Your curse has everything to do with this!" Gairynzvl's voice became a deep growl as his vexation mounted. Flexing his wings aggressively, he continued before the Celebrant could formulate a retort. "If you had not used a Forbidden Curse, I would not have needed to recover my strength and the Prevailation could have been performed this afternoon."

Ayla listened in rising dread as the two malefey continued to argue, circling each other menacingly. Mardan retorted just as caustically, "If you had undergone the Rite this afternoon, you would be in no condition to defend yourself from a Legion of Reviled tonight."

"I would be much safer than I am right now."

Mardan stood silent, returning the Dark Ones hostile stare with confusion glinting in the cerulean fire of his eyes. Gairynzvl hissed in exasperation and explained himself more thoroughly. "I have closed a portal on my own Legion. Do you think they are pleased with me? They are not coming here tonight in search of childfey or shefey. They are in search of me and when they find me, since I am not transformed, they will be able to take me back to the Uunglarda." At his mention of the realm of the Reviled, Mardan winced, beginning to understand the Dark One's logic. The Reviled could abduct Fey children, but they could not carry off adult Fey of the Light. However, having not successfully undergone The Prevailation, Gairynzvl was, as yet, one of their own and as a Dark Fey he could be forcibly returned to their vile realm.

"Do you have any comprehension what they will do to me, a traitor, once they have me?"

Mardan's steely gaze softened briefly as he considered, but he shook his head without speaking, unsure if he even wanted to know.

"First they will induce VarPrinsqua, the Curse of Endurance, so no matter what they do to me I will not lapse into unconsciousness out of pain or exhaustion," Gairynzvl continued in a dire tone, the glint in his glare betraying his fear as well as his anger. Ayla could not defend herself from the images these thoughts stirred in him, which he inadvertently shared with her. He had witnessed the deaths of several Dark Fey who suffered similar circumstances and he knew the horror that awaited him should they capture him unchanged. "Then they will torture me in ways you cannot imagine and I cannot describe, but your curse of pain will seem a summer's breeze by comparison."

Tears slipped over Ayla's cheeks as she listened and saw in her mind's eyes images of such horror that made her sick with fear. Hearing her weeping, Gairynzvl turned to glare at her, exasperated by her shifting sentiments. His emotions roiled unchecked and his tone turned into a deep growl. "Ayla!"

She gasped and flinched away from him, but Mardan grasped him by the shoulders and turned him back to face him with a jerk. "She cannot help it. It is your anger that distresses her... as well as mine."

Knocking his hands away viciously, Gairynzvl grasped him by the throat and cursed in Dlalth fluently. His frustration was rapidly taking control of him, yet before Mardan had time to defend himself Ayla shouted at them crossly.

"Stop it! Both of you!"

Ferocious crimson and infuriated cerulean turned to her as both malefey paused in surprise.

"What is wrong with you? The Legion will be here in minutes and you stand there bickering?" Stalking toward them with a rush of authoritative energy, although they both dwarfed her diminutive stature, she shoved them apart from each other and stood glaring up at them with her hands upon her hips and her expression, which had just been bleak with dread and tears, now as fiery as their own. "What is our plan? "she demanded, glaring at them both impatiently and they could not retain their mutual aggression at the sight of her. Looking back at each other, Gairynzvl shook his head. He was still angry, but realized it was neither the time nor place to debate with the Celebrant. Mardan glanced up the hallway at the light emanating from the room where the mirror stood blazing and queried in a contemplative tone.

"What did you do to the mirror?"

Gairynzvl twisted to glare at him, anticipating further accusations. He responded brusquely that he had closed it to crossing, his tone of voice clearly indicating that a Celebrant ought to know without having to ask, yet Mardan pressed him for specific details. "How did you close it? What incantation did you use?"

Ayla watched them both, at her patience's limit with their quarreling and ready to intervene again should such action be required.

"Illuminaryth," Gairynzvl answered simply, to which Mardan nodded as if he had already suspected as much and approved. Reaching for Ayla, he stepped towards the hallway even as the echo of a discordant horn pealed through the darkening forest. Instantly Gairynzvl turned toward the now well secured door, his wings flexing in preparation for battle. "They have found us," he said with certainty.

Mardan nodded and gestured for him to follow them up the hall. "Ayla, Quiroth. Quickly," he instructed with marked urgency and, although she cringed, she did not hesitate to rush toward her cabinet of simples and remedies in the far corner of the room to take from it a bottle filled with an amber liquid. Even as she did so, Celebrant turned to Dark Fey to hastily explain his strategy. "The mirror's light will not diminish and cannot be extinguished; therefore, it is the safest place for us. We must barricade ourselves within that room and wait for daylight to return." His logic was sound, but upon hearing his words, Gairynzvl blenched and Ayla stopped in her tracks, shaking her head fiercely.

"He cannot withstand the Light, Mardan. It will kill him!"

The Celebrant shook his head, moving again toward the small room only a few feet away from which spilled sparkling, brilliant light. "It will not kill him if we protect him."

"Covering me will not solve the problem. I will be in darkness beneath whatever you use and will be taken instantly," Gairynzvl retorted impatiently, but

Mardan fixed his crystalline gaze upon the visibly hesitant Dark One and spoke in a more bolstering tone.

"No, we cannot cover you. You must stand before the mirror. However, I will stand in front of you and shield you from as much light as I can."

Ayla shook her head once again and Gairynzvl cringed, but the horn calls from the dark forest were growing louder and he knew he had little choice. Returning to the Dark One's side, Mardan gazed into his crimson eyes apologetically. "It is not a perfect solution, I admit, and it will not be painless. I cannot shield you completely and, as a result, you will be forced to tolerate whatever light reaches you throughout the entire night or face the Legion." Never in his life had he seen fear in a Dark One, yet it was plain to see in Gairynzvl's expression and could not be denied. Turning to gaze back at Ayla, Mardan continued with a cunning edge in his voice. "Ayla will aid you. She will share her strength and endurance with you and when she has need of it, she will take mine from me. We shall endure together , to fortify our strength, we must all drink the Quiroth."

Turning to look upon the bottle she held in her hands, Gairynzvl shook his head uncertainly. "What is Quiroth?" Ayla grimaced and shuddered, looking down at the bottle of amber liquid she held with evident abhorrence.

"It is dreadful, that is what it is," she answered lightly, to which Mardan nodded, but added more informatively that it was a concoction of blended herbals, simples and minerals that would strengthen and fortify the one who drank of it. Although it did, indeed, taste bitter and was distinctly unpalatable, it worked well and it was not necessary to drink a great deal in order to receive its lasting benefits. Gairynzvl's expression betrayed his unconvinced estimation of such a claim, but even as he attempted to query further, a loud shout in guttural and undistinguished Dlalth rang from the garden outside, making each of them jump in alarm.

Rushing to the boudoir where the mirror stood blazing its incandescent light, they hurried inward and secured the door behind them, adding an additional barricade by pushing a large armoire in front of the door. Even as they did so, discordant blats and bugles from unharmonious horns echoed round the small cottage clearly indicating that the Legion were significant enough in number to have already encircled the cote. Ayla listened with mounting apprehension, attempting to disconnect herself from the horde just outside her once tranquil home, but their collective ferocious energy and hedonistic intentions were overwhelming. Trembling visibly, she gasped out loud and nearly dropped the bottle of Quiroth she carried.

Stepping closer to her quietly, Gairynzvl reached out slowly and took the precious vessel from her shaking hands, passing it to Mardan before he did something neither she nor her Celebrant lover anticipated. Drawing her into his arms with surprising tenderness, he hugged her close and spoke to her quietly through thought alone to reassure her. As long as they remained in the light of the mirror they had little to fear, yet he knew her concerns did not rest entirely upon herself. She had shared his memories and felt the fear and revulsion he had experienced at the traitor's execution he had earlier recalled. As a result, she knew what fate awaited him should the Legion succeed in taking him.

A thunderous clamor ensued outside the cottage door as every member of the Legion started shouting, clashing their weapons, hurling stones and branches against the exterior of the small house, and blaring their horns in a deliberate exhibition of force. Unconcerned that their raucous din would certainly draw the attention of the Fey Guard, they continued for long minutes while, within the cottage, Mardan's anxious cerulean gaze briefly locked with apprehensive crimson. Ayla cringed, covering her ears with trembling hands.

Mardan opened the Quiroth first and tipped the bottle over his lips hastily. Closing his eyes, he shuddered at the vile taste of the contents, but swallowing an ample quantity before shaking his head in revulsion and passing the bottle to Gairynzvl. He stared at it hesitantly before taking it, watching the fair Fey closely to perceive any outward sign of the concoctions efficacy, but, although Mardan flexed his vast wings powerfully and moved to stand directly before the blazing mirror, he could not distinguish any change in him. Ayla looked up at him with evident displeasure and stepped back, waiting for him to drink before she would as well, but he stared at the bottle many indecisive moments before raising it slowly to his lips.

Outside, the pounding became louder as if every member of the horde now stood, kicking and hammering upon the walls. The created such a fearsome noise that Ayla shrank from the sounds, squeezing her eyes tightly closed and pressing her hands over her ears, but the din was too great. Gairynzvl released her from his grasp, concentrating on pouring as little of the Quiroth into his mouth as he could manage. At the first taste of it, he turned his head sharply and spat in disgust, unable to force himself to swallow the pungent, earthy tasting liquid.

Immediately, Mardan rebuked him. "Drink it, Dark One! It is life!"

Gairynzvl glared back at him with a repulsed grimace and shook his head. "Even though it tastes like death?"

Mardan laughed in spite of the urgency of the moment and nodded. Tipping the bottle of amber liquid hurriedly past his lips, Gairynzvl drank all he could manage, swallowed hard against the acrid taste and smell and shoved the bottle toward Ayla vigorously, anxious to be rid of it. She took it from him far less enthusiastically. Gazing down at the bottle with evident disconcertion, she drank quickly and replaced the cork stopper while grimacing repeatedly. Had the situation been less dire she would never have ingested even a mouthful of the horrid tasting brew, but as she tapped the cork back into place securely and set the bottle aside the horde doubled their vigorous assault.

Their rancorous calls rose to a crescendo so loud that Ayla doubled over in fear, wrapping her arms over her head in a final effort to block out the uproar, but to no avail. Then deathly silence ensued, which was far more unnerving than the racket the Legion had just created. Straining to hear any indication of their movements, the three stood statuesque and even as Mardan motioned quietly for Gairynzvl to come and stand within the direct streaming light of the mirror, the noise of a resounding crash filled the small room. Cheering and laughing followed, much closer than before, making it apparent that the horde had broken down the locked front door and were now inside the cottage.

"They will break open every door in search of us," Gairynzvl asserted with confidence while hesitantly stepping into the full glare of the mirror's light. He was far too familiar with the Legion's tactics to remain standing half in the shadows. The instantaneous sting that penetrated every unprotected inch of his body at the radiant light's touch brought a hiss of discomfort from him and he raised a hand to shield his eyes as he turned his back to the mirror. Moving as close as he could to the emanating pane of shattered glass, Mardan watched the shadow he cast carefully, shifting his stance and altering the position of his wings to screen Gairynzvl as much as he was able, but the two Fey so closely resembled each other in stature that there was no way for him to protect the Dark One entirely.

Chaos echoed from the parlor as the Legionnaires wreaked havoc upon the room, overturning furniture, shattering anything breakable against the walls and tearing curtains while cursing and jeering in spiteful glee at the destruction they caused. Scratching the walls deeply with swords and hurling battle axes against timbers, they created such mayhem that some of their own ranks were unintentionally wounded as a result, although they did not allow such an occurrence to diminish their fervor.

Ayla listened in horror as her life's treasures were ripped and smashed, mocked and defiled. Mardan spoke her name quietly, wanting to comfort her, but unwilling to step away from the mirror and allow its full light to rush over Gairynzvl who had crouched down with his back to the light and wrapped his wings round himself protectively. Looking at them both, she shook her head and stepped forward waveringly. The detestable amusement of the Legion was overwhelming, but she was aware of resentment and anger as well and she did not know how to feel. She remembered the misery and anguish Gairynzvl had shared with her. She recalled how he had been forced to do things he did not wish to do and wondered if these Dark Ones who were destroying her home struggled as he had.

Moving to stand before Mardan, she turned and added what little shade she could create to the shadow they cast over Gairynzvl. Their joined silhouette protected him from the full glare of light while at the same time permitting just enough illumination to wash over him to keep him from falling into darkness. Darkness beckoned the Reviled, yet no corner of the boudoir stood without brilliant light. It was a situation that was both a blessing and a curse.

Like a swarm of persistent angry bees, the light that snaked through the irregular shadow cast over him, stung Gairynzvl repeatedly. Although he tried to think about the furious horde seeking retribution and the pain they would inflict upon him should he surrender to his desire to draw shadow around himself in protection, there was no way to ignore the torment of the light. He listened as heavy footsteps came towards the room from the hall and as the Legionnaire on the other side stopped and shuffled abruptly away while cursing in his own guttural language at the streaming light pouring into the corridor from under the door. A heavy bang thudded against the door, as if the Dark One had viciously punched the panel in anger before he backed away, yet his discovery brought others who also cursed in irate, fluent Dlalth. Their combined violence forced the tears Ayla attempted to hold at bay to finally fall over her pale cheeks.

Mardan reached out to lay his hand upon her shoulder reassuring, but it was Gairynzvl's voice she heard in her mind telling her that it would be all right, assuring her that the light would protect them, and explaining that it was for this very reason he had chosen to use the Illuminaryth Incantation on the mirror. The light the charmed mirror now produced was far too concentrated for most Legionnaires, whose fierce devotion to the Reviled's iniquitous ideology made them vastly more susceptible to the Light than a common Dark Fey. A Legionnaire's separation from the Light determined how little he could bear its radiant illumination and most could not abide one tenth the intensity he could tolerate because he still revered the Light and was not far from it in his essence.

He was a Dark Fey, however, in spite of his deep desire not to be, and the Light remained a torment. Gasping audibly at the increasing pain he felt, Gairynzvl shifted uncomfortably and reached out with one hand to steady himself. Inadvertently exposing himself to its full force, he hissed at the sensation that felt like thrusting his hand into an intensely burning open flame and, although he resumed his previously hunched position hastily, the sound penetrated the closed portal. The voices on the other side of the door fell abruptly silent. Ayla covered her mouth with her hands, staring down at him in terror and listening inwardly as he cursed his foolishness in equally fluent Dlalth as those who stood outside the door. Although Mardan was ignorant of his self-condemnation, he shook his head at his carelessness and braced his stance for what he felt certain would come next.

"Gairynzvl." From outside the door a hideous, growling voice called his name tauntingly. He froze instinctively, recognizing the voice of the Legion Centurion and shuddering involuntarily. "Gairynzvl." He repeated, slightly more urgently. Then silence stretched taut for long minutes. "Gairynzvl!" The shout came loudly and the deep tone of the Centurion's voice caused the huddled Dark One to cower into an even tighter knot, curling his wings around himself fearfully. This was the Centurion who had commanded the unit charged with executing the last traitor seeking to escape the Dlalth. The same commander who had forced the young, rebellious Gairynzvl to stand motionless and watch while his precise, methodical cruelty had doled out such horrific torture that it took the unfortunate Dark One named a traitor many, long agonizing hours to finally breathe his last.

An excessively loud crash shook the room as the Legionnaires took to breaking down the door with zeal, the unexpectedly horrendous sound drawing a scream from Ayla in spite of the steadying hands Mardan laid upon her shoulders. Stretching out his wings to their fullest, Gairynzvl rose from his crouched position to face the door and his assailants, fully aware that they would not be able to rush in and grab him, but uncertain to what extent they could take action. Bang after bang jolted through the room, as if the Legion was careful to make as much noise and take as long as possible in breaking through the portal to instill greater fear in their . Their tactic was successful.

Awaiting his fate with mounting apprehension, Gairynzvl twisted round to glance back at Ayla, his expression fierce and guarded, but when he saw the terror plainly evident upon her delicate features and saw her visible tremors his immediate reaction was one of compassion, which he did not anticipate. He knew he was the cause of her fear and the source of animosity for the Legion. If it were not for him, they would never have come to attack her tranquil home and destroy everything she held dear. Softly he apologized to her through his thoughts, uncertain if she would perceive him over the raucous din of the Legion, but she turned her tearful gaze to his and shook her head.

With a final crash, the oaken portal gave way, colliding loudly with the armoire resting up against it, but this barricade was hurled aside vengefully as if it were a small toy as several Legionnaires pressed into the small room. With the blockade cleared, the full impact of the mirror's luminescence streamed out into the hallway, forcing back the initial foray of Reviled who shouted and cursed in surprised pain and Gairynzvl could not suppress a satisfied grin at their suffering, but his miniscule victory was short lived.

Hurling several subordinates out of his way, the Centurion stalked menacingly into the room, drawing a great shadow about himself as protection against the radiant light of the mirror and even Mardan could not suppress a shudder of trepidation at the sight of him. Baleful and remorselessly glaring, his face was gaunt and hollowed like a skull and his gleaming, sinister stare was amber fire. He stood nearly seven and a half feet tall and rippled with sinew and armor, dwarfing both Mardan and Gairynzvl by a full fifteen inches; yet his wings were truly terrifying. Heavy with barbed talons and implanted spines of jagged metal, they were an imposing weapon that reached nearly twenty feet from wingtip to wingtip.

Stalking forward into the incandescent light, he watched with great satisfaction as the Fey of the Light trembled at his approach, but his insidious stare pierced the Dark One standing in their asymmetrical shadow. Pausing, he showed them a hideous, yellow-toothed grin and nodded with recognition. "Ah yes, Gairynzvl," he growled in a rasping tone. "Now it all makes sense to me. I cannot say I'm surprised to discover it's you I've been sent to reclaim or that you've enlisted the aid of paltry Lighters. But what have you done here?"

As he spoke, Ayla could sense Gairynzvl's dread, though he stood motionless and neither trembled nor balked at the fearsome Centurion's advance upon him, but when the Centurion turned to gaze more directly at the mirror and, consequently, at her as well as Mardan, a surge of monumental fear washed over her like a wave. It drowned her and robbed her breath so she was left gaping and trembling. He glared at them for long moments, his expression as cold as a demon's and he seemed content to allow his stare to intimidate them, but the cracked mirror and shimmering light it produced drew his attention at last. "The Illuminaryth Incantation?" he snarled derisively, turning back to look upon Gairynzvl more threateningly. "Did you really think this pathetic spell would protect you?"

Gairynzvl shuddered, the threat sending a torrent of doubt through him, but Mardan spoke out unexpectedly; his years of training as a Celebrant standing in defiance of the Centurion's intimidation. "You have no power here, Dark One. Take your Legion and depart before The Guard comes to ensnare you all." His strong, assured tone made the massive Reviled One turn his head and a gleam of amusement glinted in his eyes as he considered the fair Fey standing before the charmed mirror that exuded despicable light. A wicked smile turned his pinched lips, revealing a hellish grin of razor-sharp yellow teeth, filed into points to make him even more ferocious.

"Celebrant, dare not speak to me again or you'll bear my wrath," he snarled belligerently, his threat causing Ayla to blench white and nearly fall in a swoon of fear, but Mardan stepped around her. Placing her into the full glow of light pouring from the mirror in order to better protect her, he moved forward to stand audaciously behind Gairynzvl. Crimson and brilliant cerulean locked briefly and for the first time Gairynzvl sought to communicate with him through thought alone, but Mardan was unable to perceive his words as Ayla was, since his gifts were not cerebral as hers were. Still, a reassuring confidence passed between them that bolstered both.

"Threaten me not, Vile Overlord!" Mardan rebuked him brazenly, stretching out his wings to their fullest. "I fear no Reviled. I say again, take your Legion and go."

In an instantaneous flurry, the Centurion rushed inward at Mardan, the vast shadow of darkness he had gathered unto himself moving like insolent fog behind him. It lagged behind him by several seconds and left him unprotected. Moving to within inches of the fair Fey, he did not notice Ayla drop to the floor and her act of fear fortuitously cast the full blaze of the mirror's light into the unprotected Dark One. A violent growl of fury and agony escaped him as the light seared into his pale flesh, leaving smoldering open wounds as if the light were caustic flame, yet he stood for a protracted moment, malevolently glaring into Mardan's unblinking eyes in spite of the torture of the light.

Unable to tolerate the strident force of illumination, even surrounded by his glowering shadow, the Centurion cursed at him in enraged Dlalth and spun about abruptly. Retreating as rapidly as he had approached, he flexed his massive barbed and studded wing, stretching it outward and catching Mardan full in the chest to hurl him backward against the far wall with imposing ferocity. Ayla screamed in terror at the unexpected attack and the Centurion laughed viciously as her as he shuffled away from the light. Although Gairynzvl turned to look at the fallen Celebrant with concern, he did not move out of the light, even when Ayla rushed to Mardan's side and the full blast of the mirror's luminescence washed over him ruthlessly.

Gritting his teeth against the searing pain that engulfed him, Gairynzvl turned to glare hatefully into the eyes of the Centurion who stood at a safer distance, bathed in cool, refreshing shadow and watching his victim's torment unsympathetically. "How long can you stand, fool?" he taunted remorselessly, watching disinterestedly as Mardan urged Ayla to return to the face of the mirror while he struggled to catch his breath and get up. It was not this interaction that interested the Centurion, though, as much as the bottle of amber liquid she pressed into her friend's hand before she raced back to the mirror and stretched out her wings to protect Gairynzvl. She was largely unsuccessful, though, as her diminutive stature and translucent wings provided little shade.

Watching with growing interest, the Centurion stepped forward cautiously as Mardan pulled the cork from the bottle and drank hastily, his telling grimace supplying all the information the Dark Fey needed.

"Quiroth!" He said with definitive anger, fully aware of the benefits the potion provided. Even as Mardan struggled to his feet and staggered forward, attempting to hand the bottle to Gairynzvl, the Centurion lashed out once again with his wing. Unbalanced by the blow he had already taken and bleeding from the cruel sting of the metal spines that had cut deeply into his flesh, Mardan was able to avoid the repeated thrust of the Centurion's vicious wing. He managed to toss the bottle to Gairynzvl, but in payment for his impudence, the Dark One swung his wing backward and caught the Celebrant unprepared.

Hurling him to the floor, the Centurion used his barbed wing to slash and pound at him continuously, taking callous delight in the injuries he inflicted until the bleeding and battered Fey of the Light escaped the reach of his wing. Crawling to the far wall, Mardan pressed himself up against the panel and gasped for breath.

"I imagine you fear me now, Celebrant," the Centurion laughed wickedly, turning his attention back to Gairynzvl with an evil sneer.

He stood defiantly in the glimmering light of the mirror, staring back at the monstrous Reviled One without blinking as he tilted the nearly half full bottle of Quiroth over his lips and drank what remained with measured determination. Lowering the bottle with deliberate leisure, he wiped his mouth with the back of his hand and tossed the empty bottle at the feet of the Centurion rebelliously. It shattered into pieces, each reflecting an additional measure of light up onto the Reviled Overlord while Gairynzvl forced back the potent need to retch at the repellent taste of the Quiroth with a malicious sneer.

Chapter Eleven

"How long can you stand, fool, without your bungling guardian" the Centurion taunted pitilessly, having so injured Mardan that he could not regain his feet or return to the mirror. Turning his head, Gairynzvl looked behind him to assess the situation, but upon seeing the Celebrant lying on his side against the wall, only semi-conscious and bleeding profusely, he grimaced worriedly. His crimson gaze moved to Ayla who was crying bitterly, but who had not abandoned her station before the face of the mirror. Their gazes locked for a brief moment, their thoughts mingling in a torrent of apprehension that needed no words and as a result of their wordless communication he knew she would not move to Mardan's side and leave him unprotected, regardless of her desperate desire to do so.

Turning back to stare impudently at the Centurion, Gairynzvl squared his shoulders and flexed his wings unhurriedly, attempting to appear as indifferent as possible to the burning effect of the light. Ayla's shadow provided a small measure of protection from the full glare of its radiance, but the light she was unable to deflect stung him mercilessly. He was not certain of the hour, but knew well enough that it was not yet the middle of night, which meant he had many hours of torment to face before the light of dawn would chase the Reviled from the cottage. He hoped his strength and the bolstering effect of the Quiroth would outlast their zeal.

Time stole by upon leaden feet. The Centurion did not venture from the shadow he had drawn thickly around himself, but leaned against the door frame and watched his quarry with seemingly endless patience while listening to the continued destruction of the cottage wrought by the unoccupied Legionnaires. He took immense pleasure in causing as much distress as he could to the shefey who so obviously owned the small cottage they were remorselessly destroying. He watched her with diligent cruelty as she stood quietly weeping at the sounds of decimation coming from all corners of her home. Gairynzvl, however, was not amused. He had been one of the destroyers many times. He knew what delight the over-mastered Legionnaires took in plundering and devastating because they had little release otherwise. The Centurion was a severe overlord who allowed few moments of enjoyment to the ones under his command. His opinion was that generosity only bred rebellion, so he kept his minions under his thumb and pressed them often to retain discipline.

An hour drew by uneventfully, then another, yet at last the Centurion yawned with evident boredom and called one of his underlings to him, speaking in a hushed tone that neither Ayla nor Gairynzvl could hear. After speaking surreptitiously, the two Dark Fey looked back at the one they were sent to reclaim with ruthless grins. Snickering derisively, the legionnaire drew a deep breath and turned towards Ayla, rubbing his hands together briskly and gathering his strength under him before he lunged upward toward the ceiling and towards her.

Shrieking in terror, Ayla covered her head and cringed to the floor as the Legionnaire snatched and grabbed at her from the ceiling where the light from the mirror was less intense. Mardan groaned prodigiously and pushed himself up from the floor where he had been slipping in and out of consciousness for well over an hour and, in spite of his wounds, staggered unsteadily to her side where he protected her with his body and glared up at the Dark Fey challengingly. Gairynzvl cursed repeatedly in Dlalth at their ruthless tactic and crouched down out of the direct, stinging glare of undeflected light pouring over him; the potency of the increased glare causing him to hiss vehemently in pain. The entire scene made the Centurion laugh heartily at the suffering he inflicted without having to move an inch or lay a finger on any of them and he watched with satisfaction as the Fey of the Light suffered.

Tired of toying with the vile assailants, Mardan raised himself up from his hunched position and glared up at the Legionnaire pressing himself to the ceiling over their heads. Stretching out his blood stained wings defiantly as he spoke in a slow, inexorable tone, he repeated the Spell of the Inflicted Pain he had used upon Gairynzvl. "Cruciavaeryn!"

Upon articulating the word, the Reviled Fey screamed in horror and crashed to the floor at their feet, writhing in agony. The Centurion's eyes grew wide in surprise, but he made no move to rescue the afflicted subordinate. Rather, he watched curiously as the underling howled and the Celebrant glared back at him coldly. Smiling, the fierce overlord was undeniably amazed at the blatant show of ferocity by so fair a Fey. "I can listen to him yowl all night. Can you, Celebrant?" the Centurion taunted callously, certain that the suffering he caused would force Mardan to retract his curse, but to his astonishment, Mardan drew himself up to his full height, arranged his wings so they once again provided sufficient shade to protect Gairynzvl, and glared back at him with a frighteningly icy glimmer in his cerulean eyes. Raising an eyebrow in fascination, the Centurion leaned back against the doorframe and smiled. "There are many hours remaining before dawn," he said with cold determination.

Breathing deeply with relief at the added shadow Mardan's wings provided, Gairynzvl twisted and looked up at the Celebrant appreciatively, his thoughts reaching out with as much focus as he could manage, hoping he would be able to ask him how he fared without the need to speak, but again he was unsuccessful. Mardan simply could not hear him. Nevertheless, Ayla could and she responded from behind her protector. "His show of strength is a ruse." The soft worry of her thoughts filled his mind and Gairynzvl turned slightly to focus on her instead. She had chosen to remain kneeling upon the floor and he could plainly see the weariness present in her amber gaze.

"He draws his strength from you?" His thoughts queried in return, already certain of her response and when she merely closed her eyes in affirmation before reaffixing him with her fatigued gaze he looked up at Mardan with concern he could not disguise. He had to do something to end this bitter conflict before he caused more irreparable harm. Standing up from his cowering position, Gairynzvl flexed his wings angrily. "You will not defeat us, Dravlug." He said in a tone Ayla had never heard from him before. Brazen and menacing, his words dripped with rebellious defiance and arrogance, but the Centurion only smiled.

"Well, well, well. It only took three hours and here you are again, the Gairynzvl I know and despise so thoroughly." His derision only served to make Gairynzvl all the more impudent as he spat back in a tone filled with even greater insolence.

"Be warned, hravclanoch," he hissed, mingling his speech with gutteral Dlalth, "the Fey Guard is already coming. If you leave now, you may yet escape to track me another day. Remain, and you will certainly face the Prison of Daylight." At the mention of this torturous chamber of execution, the Centurion's gaze showed the slightest indication of nervousness, for good reason.

The Prison of Daylight was nothing to scoff about. It had claimed many a Reviled One's life and their passing was agonizing and slow. The Prison was little more than a cage of glittering, golden iron that stood in a bright clearing where no shade could reach, where no water flowed and where no respite could be taken from full exposure to the sun and its lethal light. The Light Loving Fey used this simple, yet horrifically effective devise to punish and execute the Reviled they captured and it became a powerful deterrent.

Yet, in spite of the possibility of suffering so dreadful a death, the Centurion smiled wickedly and stepped closer to Gairynzvl boldly, drawing his cooling shadow with him into the light of the mirror. Speaking in full Dlalth, his rasping words escaped the comprehension of the two who listened, but Gairynzvl understood him perfectly and his pale complexion drained of any colour at hearing his words. Both seeing and feeling his terror, Ayla immediately questioned what the Dark One said, but Gairynzvl would not repeat his words. Shaking his head, he did not even look at her. Instead, he gathered his strength and stood up taller and more defiantly than before, staring back into the Centurions eyes with greater malice before he yawned in his face and turned to investigate Mardan's condition.

He stood with little outward indication of distress, but had closed his eyes, perhaps to block out the continued screaming of the legionnaire scrabbling at his feet or perhaps so the Centurion would not see the truth of his situation betrayed in his expressive eyes. He could have been trying to focus his energy and balance or he could simply have been exhausted. Regretting his choice to drink all the Quiroth himself, Gairynzvl stepped closer to the Celebrant and reached to take hold of Mardan's arm questioningly.

When their gazes met, the truth was powerfully evident. Every ounce of strength he currently possessed came from Ayla, yet there remained an insolent gleam in his reddened eyes that made the Dark Fey smirk with satisfaction. He knew the Centurion watched them closely, but since Mardan was unable to hear his thoughts, Gairynzvl had no alternative but to speak, although he did so in the lowest voice he could use. "This must end," he said quietly. Mardan closed his eyes in agreement and then reaffixed him with a curious gaze, waiting for his suggestion without a word. Ayla waited as well, her attention piqued, although she did not move and by doing so risk losing the focus of her thoughts from aiding Mardan. Gairynzvl looked past the wavering Celebrant to her, querying without a word if the Fey Guard were really on their way. It was a fact only she would truly know. Her subtle nod of assent was all he required to set his plan into motion.

"Release him," he spoke quietly yet firmly, looking down at the writhing Dark One at their feet, weary of his howling. "Then, no matter what occurs, stay behind me against the wall. I will bear the Light until the Guard arrives." His tone expressed his determination with finality and, although his friends looked at each other with hesitation, Mardan's deteriorating condition and Ayla's growing weakness made arguing with his tactics pointless.

Looking down at the legionnaire unsympathetically, Mardan recanted the Spell of Inflicted Pain and released him from his agony, but even as he did so Gairynzvl stooped and grasped him by his throat, hauling him up from the floor in an impressive show of strength. Turning then to face the mirror, he held the shrieking legionnaire in front of him, clutching his throat tightly while pressing the twelve inch spine on one of his wing into the underside of his chin. The other wing's spine he thrust into the soft flesh beneath his ribs, just below his heart. Effectively immobilized, the legionnaire had little choice but to bear the full, radiating glare of the light pouring from the mirror, By blocking most of the glow from reaching Gairynzvl, he unwillingly protecting him.

"Now, hravclanoch," Gairynzvl began in an intractable tone, using the same insulting Dlalth word he had used previously, "flee or face the Prison of Daylight. It's your choice. I can stand here all night."

The Centurion stepped forward menacingly, his vicious gaze clearly betraying his desire to tear his opponent's flesh from his bones, yet even as he stalked forward with a measured pace the clear, vibrant peals of fluted horns rang out from the surrounding forest. The Dark Fey crashing and smashing throughout the house shouted in dread, recognizing the jubilant sound as the horns of the Fey Guard who were much closer than they had believed. Cursing in vulgar Dlalth, the Centurion halted his forward progress and snarled in rage, glaring hatefully at Gairynzvl whose sneer had shifted to a devilish grin.

Ayla turned to stare at the wall, stretching her senses outward to determine how many of The Guard had come and breathing a great sigh of relief when she determined there were many rather than few. Gazing worriedly into Mardan's glassy stare, she whispered reassuringly to him, but her soft words enraged the Centurion. Cheated of his victory, he lashed out with his wingtip at the pair huddled on the floor at the base of the far wall. The fearsome spins of his wing scraped plaster from the panels and cracked floorboards as he stabbed and slashed at them repeatedly. Gathering what strength remained in him, Mardan raised himself from the floor, pressing Ayla against the wall behind him in order to protect her and taking the full brunt of the Centurion's ruthless attack.

Prepared for the Centurion's callous assault against the helpless, rather than facing a fully capable foe, Gairynzvl closed his eyes, stretched out his free hand, and spoke an incantation in the High Language of Celebrae, the language of The Ancients. His deep voice rang out clear against the crashing calamity the Centurion caused, but while Ayla listened in amazement to the words she barely understood, Mardan comprehended their meaning fully and opened his eyes in amazement to stare at Gairynzvl with horror.

Outside the horns of the Fey Guard rang out in closer proximity, filling the cottage with their bright sound and lifting the spirits of all who heard them. Reviled Ones began to scatter in haste, shrinking into the darkness opposite the sound, although some drew weapons and stood their ground and a few plunged out the front door in reckless abandon, preferring the thrill of battle and certain death to the torment of continued captivity.

"Gairynzvl, No!" Mardan shouted over the din, hoping to dissuade him from his chosen course, but the Dark One he'd come to consider a comrade only opened his eyes and gazed with fixed determination at the Celebrant, shaking his head slowly. Uncertain what was happening, the Centurion ceased his attack long enough to search the fair Fey's expression curiously, but when he received nothing useful from him, he turned to glare once again at the one he had been sent to reclaim. Opening his mouth, he attempted to rebuke him, but to his dismay he found he could not utter a sound. His breathing had been choked by an unseen force. He could neither speak nor draw breath and the acute panic that descended upon him was the only thing that made Gairynzvl pause.

"Do not use the Suplaythus Incantation, Gairynzvl. It is a horror you will never be able to live with and one Ayla should never see." Mardan spoke slowly, emphasizing his words with heartfelt assurance. "You are a Dark One no longer, Gairynzvl; you never were. Do not take up their ruthlessness now."

Crimson and cerulean met in a stare that no longer held the malice, hate and distrust that had been so prominent only hours before. Shaking his head purposefully, Mardan's expression pleaded with him wordlessly, in spite of the pain he felt from the Centurion's vicious attacks and the spatters of his own blood that stained the wall and floor. The Incantation he had begun was forbidden and for good reason, as it stifled its victim through an agonizing inversion of their being beginning with the loss of breath and ultimately splaying them open without the use of any weapon. Gairynzvl contemplated warily, returning his crimson glare to the Centurion who stood grasping his throat, an evil leer twisting his features even as his eyes grew dark. This overlord had been the cause of so much suffering, his own as well as other Legionnaires, and his brutality was inescapable. The thought of retribution spurred Gairynzvl to continue speaking while at the same time Mardan's warning rang in his thoughts. He slowed his speech as he reconsidered his chosen course another time.

Outside, the strident horn calls of the Fey Guard rang out sharply, mingling with shouts and clashes of weaponry as the Fey of the Light met in battle the rush of Dark Fey pouring from the house. The Legionnaire Gairynzvl held in his iron-like grasp howled in agony as the light from the mirror suddenly doubled in intensity, as if reflecting the glow of so many glimmering aura from the Fey Guard had magnified its outpouring of radiance. Exasperated and weary beyond measure of the corruption and viciousness he had been forced to endure for so many years, Gairynzvl turned sharply and hurled his prisoner directly into the Centurion, watching with satisfaction as they tumbled in a chaos of Dlalth curses and flailing limbs.

Dropping his hands to his sides, he stared with hatred at the Centurion, but he did not continue the incantation he had begun and in his silence, the unfinished spell lost its potency and faded, leaving the hulking Reviled One gasping and spluttering upon his hands and knees with his fearsome wings splayed out upon the floor. His comrade gathered his senses, took one final glance over his shoulder at his leader and fled, yowling like a wounded dog.

As the intense light of the mirror washed over him, Gairynzvl cringed and moved to seek shelter from the luminous glare, stretching out his wings to block as much of the forceful blaze as he could manage, but as he did so, the Centurion rushed at him like an enraged bear. His metal-spiked wings slashed, his studded-leather gloved hands hammered, and his viciously pointed teeth ripped cruelly. Gairynzvl barely had time to double over in a protective huddle before the massive Centurion overpowered him and pressed him to the floor as he attacked with ferocious brutality.

Ayla screamed in blood-chilling horror as she watched helplessly, both feeling and sensing Gairynzvl's pain and fear as he tried desperately to defend himself. Mardan struggled to get to his feet, intending to help in any manner he could, but after bearing the full force of the Centurion's attack not once, but twice, he had little strength remaining. Instead, he turned to look at Ayla with an uncompromising expression, insisting that she release him from her aid so she might provide, somehow, for their friend. "He needs you more than I." Not waiting for her to argue, he reached to his side and handed her his golden dagger, crafted by the Celebrant High Priests themselves and named Gieldyth, Bane of all Dark Fey. She stared at the gilded implement of death with dread, filled with hesitancy and doubt, yet when Gairynzvl screamed under the continued lash of the Centurion's remorselessly rending wings she gathered her courage about her like armor and raised herself to her feet.

Drawing back her strength from what she had given Mardan and standing in the full light of the mirror, Ayla's aura glowed with a vibrancy it had never before possessed. Her fears stifled and her courage bolstered by anger over the assaults on those for whom she cared, as well as the destruction of her home, she drew herself up to her full height. Although the Centurion still dwarfed her by nearly two feet, she pointed the dagger at him and repeated the word she had heard Gairynzvl use twice before. "Hravclanoch!"

Grasping Gairynzvl by the throat to discourage any retaliatory action he might take, the Centurion turned his head slowly to stare with amusement at the insignificant shefey standing boldly before him, his amber gaze locking with hers and causing her to shudder so violently that the golden blade she pointed at him tottered in her grasp and threatened to fall to the floor. He laughed at her paltry show of bravery and stretched his bloodied wing outward toward her, as if to flick an inconsequential insect from his view, but when the jagged, barbed spines of his wing came close to her, she lashed out with unexpected ferocity.

Honed to perfection, the glimmering blade effortlessly slashed through the membrane of his wing, entirely dismembering the weapon he directed at her. The weapon was so sharp that he took no notice of her action until the clattering sound of metal upon the floor drew his attention. When he saw what she had done, his anger rose to an insurmountable intensity. Growling at her in a verbal onslaught of Dlalth profanity, he leapt from his kneeling position over top of Gairynzvl and lunged at her. In his haste, however, he neglected to consider her position directly before the magnified light of the mirror that was spilling out its radiance with double its previous intensity in response to the

Fey Guard just outside. Unable to draw his snakelike shadow of darkness along with him in so rapid a movement, he unwittingly exposed himself a second time to the battering light of the mirror.

Screaming in fury and agony, the Centurion clamped his massive hand around her supple throat as he closed his massive wings around them both in an attempt to protect himself from the scalding light. Shrieking in terror, Ayla raised the golden blade reflexively, her only thought freedom and breath, and, in spite of her lack of any formal training in combat, she succeeded in so deeply lacerating his wrist that he withdrew his grasp from her immediately in the fear of entirely losing his hand. Hissing at her like a gargantuan viper, he lunged forward and sunk his teeth into the hand that held the glittering blade, forcing her to drop the razor-sharp weapon. As it fell tumbling toward the floor, the cutting edge severed the breadth of his dragon-like pinion and lodged itself deeply into bone.

Howling in rage, the Centurion pummeled her into the floor and raised his other wing, shifting his bulk in spite of his wounds and his visibly searing flesh to direct the jagged spine of his other wing at her chest. Even as he paused to aim his strike with deliberate cruelty, Gairynzvl purshed himself upward from the floor, wrapped both arms around the enormous wing poised to deliver a killing blow and leaned backward with all the strength he possessed, beating his wings in a backward, upward motion forcefully to triple the counterbalance of his weight. His impeding action met with a verbal assault of additional vulgarity when the Centurion lumbered sideways, thrown off balance by his full weight as he hung from his wingtip.

Swinging at him with a tightly clinched fist, the leader of the Reviled once again contented himself with battering the traitorous Fey he had been sent to reclaim. Intent upon depriving him of his life if he could not return him to the Uunglarda, he battered him mercilessly and there was little Gairynzvl could do to protect himself from the relentless attack. With his attention diverted, however, the Centurion turned his back on Ayla, who lay on the floor with her senses reeling, and concentrated his energy into murderous intent. Nothing would stop him.

Nothing, until he felt the golden blade ripped from his wing violently. Then he paused long enough to swing his head around to seek the new assailant, his glowing amber gaze locking with brilliant cerulean long enough to see the fair Celebrant standing over him, bloodied wings outstretched as he raised the dripping blade over his head.

Ayla screamed. Gairynzvl opened his eyes, gasping for breath.

"I fear *no* Reviled!" Mardan spat with deliberate inflection before he brought the blade down forcefully, sinking it up to the hilt in the vile overlord's throat. Turning the blade with purposeful action, he yanked it back out again, sideways.

The garbled splutter the Centurion emitted bubbled in the rush issuing from his throat. His eyes bulged in shock and pain, yet even as he reached upward toward the Celebrant's glowing aura, he leaned backward precariously, darkness claiming his glowing amber gaze. Gairynzvl scrambled from beneath his massive form as he crashed downward, dead before he hit the floor.

The clash of battle from the forest echoed with shouts of Dlalth vulgarity and Fey Guard wrath, yet within what remained of the boudoir, silence prevailed. Exhausted, Mardan dropped the golden blade and fell to his knees, the dimness of unconsciousness swirling at the edges of his vision. Gairynzvl lay on the floor under the gleam of the mirror, breathless and bleeding, unable to escape the burning sensation of the light. Tears fell silently from his crimson gaze as he listened with unguarded remorse to the sound of Ayla's weeping. Then voices filled his mind; voices that questioned; voices that blamed, voices that pleaded in softly tender tones. He could not find the strength to rise, but he opened his eyes long enough to see three tall Fey Guards in full golden armor standing over them.

They were speaking to Ayla, but a loud rushing sound filled his hearing and he could not perceive their words. The intense pain from the light of the mirror consumed every ounce of vigor he still possessed, but even as he tried desperately to get up one of the Guards moved to the mirror and drew his golden sword. Another lifted Mardan from the floor, speaking a hushed incantation as he carried him from the room. Ayla was pleading with the third, moving to stand between him and Gairynzvl as she sought to make him understand that the young Dark Fey was not the enemy. Her words eluded him, but Gairynzvl could sense her panic and determination. The Guard standing before the mirror pointed towards the door resolutely; nevertheless, she knelt beside the Dark One lying upon the floor, moaning in pain, and covered him with her body.

"I shall not leave him. Touch him, Bryth, and you will understand," she insisted with emphatic resolve, turning her head to address her thoughts hastily to Gairynzvl, explaining that this Fey had the gift of Discernment and he should not hide his thoughts from him. Swimming in a haze of pain and fatigue, Gairynzvl could hardly have prevented him even if he had wished to. The tall Fey Guard looked down on him doubtfully, but stooped and removed his glove to lay his hand upon the Dark Fey's chest, closing his eyes briefly to discern his essence and it only took a moment for him to realize that everything Ayla was desperately trying to tell them was true. Turning his head, he looked at the Guard standing before the mirror and nodded, then looked back at Gairynzvl.

"We shall tend your wounds; have no fear." Then he gathered the young Fey in his arms, lifting him from the floor and moving quickly toward the door, out of the lethal radiance streaming over him. As they abandoned the battleground, Gairynzvl watched the Guard before the mirror curiously as he turned, raised his enormous blade over his head, spun round in a momentum gathering motion and struck the mirror with such force that it exploded violently.

Light burst outward in a golden glare of luminescence that permeated the cottage and streamed outward into the dark forest, filling the entire vale with radiance that lingered in a spectacular blaze and did not fade for many moments. Yet when the illumination subsided, Gairynzvl felt a gentle hand clasp his and heard Ayla's soft voice in his mind, her tones filled with worry and reassurance as the cool touch of darkness tried to claim him.

Opening his eyes wearily, he found her amber gaze locked on him and looked upon love for the first time.

Chapter Twelve

The hours of darkness stretched on, filled with shadows and vague whisperings as all three young Fey were tended by the Healers of the Temple amid the quiet environs of the Temple Healing Wards. The three unlikely warriors had been given quiet rest under protective watch. Many of the rogue Dark Fey who had scattered when the Guard first arrived were, as yet, unaccounted for and their safety could have been in jeopardy. The night deepened, then faded as lavender predawn sparked the horizon with fair and then brilliant shades of roses and when the splendor of the sun stepped beyond the sill of the world, its grace was magnified by choruses of birds. The three combatants, survivors of the unprecedented battle that had shaken the vale through the dim hours, slept on, exhausted and sorely in need of recovering their strength.

It was after the noontide when Ayla finally stirred, waking to find herself on a bed that stood between the beds of her accepted companion, Mardan, which was common knowledge, and Gairynzvl as well. The young Dark Fey filled the Fey Guard who stood watch with skeptical curiosity, as well as those members of family and friends who had come to visit them after the light of day revealed the decimation of Ayla's small cottage. Without opening her eyes, Ayla listened to the hushed voices around her, not amazed that their conversations should be filled with concerns, disbelief, and accusations that made her wish with all her heart that none of them had come at all. Instead she wished she could remain peacefully nestled between her two protectors and dream of sweeter days.

It was the thought of those sweeter days that finally made her open her eyes and get up as she recalled the reason for Gairynzvl's presence beside her in the first place: his desire to undergo the Prevailation. Such a request would surely meet opposition now that the Fey Guard were involved and with them the High

Celebrant Priests who would have no reason to allow such a rite to take place. It would take much convincing on her part and she could not be certain that Mardan would support her, support them, now that Gairynzvl's presence was no longer a secret. His arrival in Jyndari had already caused enough calamity and commotion to fuel resistance against his remaining in their otherwise peaceful village. Surely the Celebrants would seek the quietest, easiest solution to the problem he presented.

Gazing upon him as he slept, she stretched out her senses cautiously to touch him. Seeking to know that he would be all right despite the battering he had taken, she let her gaze fall over his many wounds, now carefully tended and bandaged. She was not surprised to discover that he was weak with fatigue and the lingering pain his injuries caused him, but she could also sense the overwhelming relief he felt at being, at long last, free from the horrors of the Reviled and their domination of him. Even in his sleep he sighed with the pleasure of long desired tranquility and safety and she could not keep herself from reaching out to touch him with her small hand, laying it carefully upon his bandaged shoulder and whispering to him through her thoughts.

"Safe at last, Gairynzvl. No longer a captive to darkness and fear." Her gentle words brought a subtle smile to his lips, even from sleep, but she withdrew her hand before her thoughts would rouse him further and turned, instead, to inspect Mardan's condition.

His wounds were far more severe than she had expected and at the sight of him, lying wrapped in more bandage than blanket, she burst into tears. He lay shivering, the warmth of the afternoon sun as well as the blanket that had been tenderly draped over him, ineffectual. His injuries and the substantial amount of blood he had lost made anything the Healers attempted futile, at best. Reaching out to touch his pale cheek, Ayla stretched forth her senses once again, waiting to sense him, searching, but his presence beside her was dim. Withdrawing her hand abruptly, she drew in several deep breaths as she tried to clear her mind of the billowing wave of emotion threatening to crash over her, and sought him again.

Laying her hand upon his cheek, which was one of few areas of his body without any bandages where she could touch him directly, she concentrated more purposefully. Seeking, asking, pausing in the silence that filled her mind, shaking her head furiously to stretch further, wait longer, but the quietness that crossed to her was deafening. Breath remained, heartbeat lingered, but the silence of his essence filled her with dread. Raising her hand from his cheek, she covered her mouth to stifle the cry of anguish that rose from the pit of her stomach. Turning away in an attempt to retain her composure, she did not notice one of the Healers who stood nearby watching her with compassion and an interest that was not quite concealed. He was aware of her particular gifts and was undeniably curious, but he said nothing when their gazes locked with mutual concern. Moving closer, he reached to touch Mardan as well, his expression thoughtful, yet even as his viridian gaze once again met hers, she shook her head.

"I cannot find him." She spoke softly, her tone filled with emotion that would not permit her to say more as tears spilled over her cheeks. Beside her, roused from sleep not only by her gentle touch upon him, but by the powerful swell of grief overwhelming her that transferred to him, Gairynzvl opened his eyes and turned his head with a moan to gaze at her uncertainly.

"Ayla?" He asked in a hushed tone, the soft sound of his voice drawing her from the pit of despair into which she was sinking. Twisting to gaze upon him with a potent combination of relief and misery, she reached for him and leaned down beside him, allowing him to enwrap her with a tender embrace. Their thoughts mingled in the quietness of the room and, though neither spoke, each knew and understood the other's concern.

"He is so quiet," she told him, fear tainting every word and every emotion she shared with him. He remained quiet, his ability to respond reassuringly because of his own fears and guilt.

"If it were not for me," he thought bitterly, but she raised her head to stare into his crimson hued eyes with firm resolve. Although she did not speak physically, her words rang with determination.

"You cannot blame yourself for something done by another."

He shook his head. "Mardan bore the Centurion's attack because he was protecting me. How can I not blame myself?"

"He bore it for me as well, Gairynzvl. Am I also to blame?" she posed her question verbally, raising herself from his warm embrace to gaze at him more directly, but he turned his head away as tears of doubt and self-recrimination escaped his resistance. She could say nothing. The ache inside her stole her voice and filled her with fear. Straightening, she wrapped a blanket round her and walked aimlessly about the room, trying to distract her thoughts. It was one of the many halls of the Temple where the Healers practiced their skills.

It was bathed in streaming light as the afternoon sun shone through a myriad windows, all shuttered at varying degrees to create ribbons and cascades of luminance that streamed down from the highly vaulted ceiling. From every corner statues of The Ancients watched in spectral silence and the only sound that could be heard was a soft splashing fountain set into one of the stone walls. Its endless cycling of crystalline water fell in small rivulets down the length of the wall, tumbling over the uneven surface in a mirror-like stream until it reached the pool at the bottom and was swept up once more.

Stopping in the ribbons of light filtering down from above, Ayla raised her bandaged hands and allowed the spilling light to warm them, wondering quietly over the golden rays that filled her with warmth and life, but did little for Mardan. Was he so far away? Would he return? Would she ever gaze into his breathtaking cerulean eyes again? As she considered, tears sprang anew and she could not help covering her face and sobbing aloud. She had treated him so unfairly!

Seeing her standing alone, the Healer who had touched Mardan and shared her worried gaze approached quietly. Without speaking a single word, he opened his arms and his broad wings in a consolatory gesture she could not refuse. He drew her close, enwrapping her within his warming, reassuring presence and she cried for long moments before the tide of her anguish abated. Looking up at him wearily, she met his viridian gaze.

"He is strong. He will return." The Healer's rich baritone voice was soft and immensely reassuring and she smiled dimly before she moved away quietly.

Late in the afternoon Gairynzvl roused himself more fully and was able to take nourishment, but the Healers would not permit him to get up lest his injuries be made worse by his impatience. Ayla joined him in his solitary meal and they spoke quietly of their concerns for their friend who had not yet stirred. Though reassured by more than one of the Healers that his wounds were not severe enough to merit their grief their quiet gazes returned to Mardan again and again.

The evening brought with it suffuse light and the warming glimmers of fires from several massive hearths that heated the Healing Wards. The environment was peaceful and soothing, but when the chanting voices of the Celebrants, who also resided within the Temple, filled the chamber with soft echoes of their evening prayers, Gairynzvl closed his eyes against the sound. "I should not be here," he muttered under his breath, his differences from the fair Fey around him painfully evident. Ayla shook her head.

"There is no better place for you to be. Is this not what you wanted, to be filled with the Light, to be made whole again?" Her words stung him as cruelly as the light from the mirror that had burned his body so remorselessly only hours before.

"Having you perform The Prevailation is one thing. This is entirely different." His answer did not satisfy.

"I cannot perform it, Gairynzvl, you know that as well as I do; as well as Mardan knew. I am not strong enough."

He hissed at her, not wishing to hear the truth in her reproach and unwilling to accept that everything he had done, everything he had suffered, had been in vain. "Then I am truly cursed." He had barely spoken the words when their conversation was interrupted by the Healer who had begun tending Mardan when the Healer with viridian eyes had taken his leave for the evening.

"You are far from being Cursed or Reviled, Young Fey." His rich voice interposed their melancholy discussion and both turned to gaze at him, one with an expression of agreement while the other frowned doubtfully. "We are full of speculation, but cannot determine how any of you survived the night. It shall be a tale worth telling when you are recovered more fully."

Gairynzvl shook his head and turned away. "I have no wish to share anything, Healer," he began somewhat petulantly and Ayla turned back to him while formulating a gentle rebuke for his insolence, but the Healer only smiled and stepped closer.

"You should reconsider, Young Fey. You will be asked to share a great many things before undergoing the Prevailation."

Again, both Ayla and Gairynzvl turned to gaze at the Healer, but this time with far greater interest and he smiled more genuinely at their honest curiosity. Moving closer still, he drew back his hood, which all the Healers wore over their heads in reverence to their task and their place within the Temple, and unfurled his broad wings in a gesture of relaxation.

"My name is Veryth," he offered unceremoniously before he paused to hear their names. His smile never faded as he proceeded to explain that he had been sent by the Elders to discuss Gairynzvl's desire to undergo the Prevailation and to answer any questions he might have about the ceremony. Never once did he indicate that the rite might not be considered, nor did he discourage the Dark

Fey in any manner. He was entirely genial and did not falter when faced with the Dark One's anti-social demeanor, but spoke openly with him about what he should expect, as well as what would be asked of him in return.

The evening darkened as the sun set and lamps were lit to illumine the chambers of the Temple. Veryth and Gairynzvl walked about the vast halls, their conversation touching on many aspects of the ritual he wished to undertake, as well as the sort of life he wished to lead once he could, once again, walk among the Fey of the Light without fear. They discussed his memories and the pain that haunted him from the many long years he had been forced to live captive to the Reviled. Never in all the hours they spoke did Veryth lay one word of accusation or blame upon him. Never once did he endeavor to make Gairynzvl uncomfortable about anything he had been forced to do while under the domination of the Dark Ones, regardless of the fact that both Fey were fully aware of what sort of atrocities they were and how brutally he had been forced to act.

Many things Gairynzvl already knew, things he had secretly researched and studied in preparation for the ritual, yet many others he did not know. He listened as carefully as his waning attention would allow while Veryth described the rite in detail and suggested several questions for him to ponder and reflect upon. They were questions he would be required to answer before the Prevailation would be performed; questions that would reveal his intentions, his motives, as well as his desires and hopes. Such requirements of honesty had never been necessary before and Gairynzvl little knew how to consider them, but Veryth assured him they would spend more time together in the days to come during which they would discuss in even greater detail these presently vexing dilemmas. He also advised him that he should not allow any of the questions given to him or contemplations about the ceremony to deny him the rest he needed. The demands of the Prevailation were intense and he would need all his strength to endure it.

Agreeing that the hour was late and seeing full well that he could not continue, Veryth bid him goodnight and quietly withdrew, leaving him in Ayla's company. As the two greeted each other with a gentle touch of their hands and their gazes locked in quietness that clearly betrayed the mingling of their thoughts, Veryth paused behind a towering pillar of stone to observe their interaction with marked curiosity before he returned to his duties. They spoke in a wordless manner that did not disturb the solemn hush of the temple hall. They spoke as the candles that had been lighted when the sun slipped below the far western horizon guttered and burned themselves out and they sat quietly in the dimness of the moonlight streaming down through the shutters. Ayla's concern for Mardan had deepened during the long hours she sat attentively by his side while Gairynzvl and Veryth spoke. She could do little to hide her apprehension, regardless of how interested she was to learn what they had discussed for so long, but Gairynzvl sat in silence.

Weary from the unfamiliar hours of extended conversation, Gairynzvl was far more interested in resting than confiding in anyone further. He had spoken in one day far more than he had in months before and all he wanted to do was to close his eyes and let the shifting chaos in his mind settle. He could dismiss her curiosity without much guilt, but he knew he should not dismiss her anxiety over Mardan in similar fashion. Uncertain, however, how to properly comfort her because he had little experience with such compassionate action, he listened quietly as she shared her thoughts and fears. She shared with him for many long moments before he shook his head and closed his eyes.

"You are tired. I should let you rest," she spoke softly, her tone filled with emotion that seemed to be stretched taut. Lifting his head that had dropped in fatigue, he gazed at her with a mixture of bewilderment and frustration in not being able to soothe her uneasiness. Entirely at a loss as to what he might say that would reassure her when he could not honestly reassure himself, he simply stared at her. In the soft moonlight, her flaxen colored hair fell softly across her shoulders, left bare by the nightdress she wore, and the tender blush of her ivory cheeks seemed to glow in the glimmering light.

Turning her head to watch Mardan, she sighed with exasperation. Shutting herself off from the emptiness she sensed whenever she attempted to reach him, she also blocked any sense of Gairynzvl beside her and was unaware of his intense stare. She needed peace. She needed to re-center herself. She needed to rest without the confusion of doubt, despair and helplessness that crested within her every time she sensed either of them.

Gairynzvl watched her silently, the hammering of his heart drowning out everything else, including his weariness. A deep yearning blazed within him that was sudden and unyielding. Reaching out slowly, he touched her bare shoulder, turning her back to face him and she gazed at him with questioning surprise. He returned her stare briefly, his thoughts a torrent of powerful, wordless emotion that washed over her with the force of a full moon's tide. Without speaking, he looked down at his hand lightly touching her bare skin and his crimson gaze darkened with a desire he could not disguise.

Guilt pressed in on his thoughts briefly. With Mardan lying so close he knew he should not feel the fervent need rushing over him, but he did not know how to conceal such an intense sensation from her when she often knew and understood his emotions better than he understood them himself. Her amber stare melted through him and her lips parted breathlessly as she became aware of his desire. She did not speak, but the sight was more than he could bear.

Grasping her shoulder more firmly, he pulled her closer, his crimson gaze focused on her mouth. She gasped, but did not pull away when he leaned nearer and, with gentleness she did not anticipate, pressed his lips against hers. He paused as their thoughts mingled intoxicatingly and his wordless request filled her mind. *Query.* He moaned softly, drawing her closer to him as her unspoken response came back to him. *Uncertainty.* Wrapping his arms about her, he allowed the fervor of his kiss to deepen. *Desire!* She shivered and leaned into his embrace. *Sigh.*

The swirling, pounding ardor that washed over her was more than she could manage. His emotions flooded over her with a force she could barely resist and she gasped aloud, entirely overwhelmed by him. He paused to lean back, gazing at her questioningly once again. His heart hammered in his chest. His passion blazed, but the uncertainty ringing in her thoughts and the shifting splash of her precarious emotions made him frown.

He wanted her. There was no way to deny it. After all the time he had spent watching her, studying her, learning how different and remarkable she was, he could not help finding her irresistible. He ached for her, yet this need inside him that was driving and pressuring him was not the same as it had always been before and the realization of this truth confounded him. His passion was real, too real, but there was another sensation mixed with the physicality of his need he had never experienced before. It was a yearning in his heart that made him lean away from her even further to stare at her, perplexed. Hunger gnawed at him ravenously, but he wanted more. He wanted more from her. What it was, however, he could not name.

Opening her eyes, she smiled at him breathlessly, having heard his inward musings and confusion. Taking his hand in hers affectionately, she leaned closer another time and kissed him gently, whispering his name softly upon his lips. "Gairynzvl."

He moaned in answer, saying nothing.

"Will you wait until the time is more right?" she asked softly. Turning his head slightly to one side he considered briefly, but even before his thoughts cleared of the desire he felt he found himself nodding and quietly agreeing. The smile she offered him and the gentle embrace and tender kiss she gave him brought a smile to his lips and caused his head to swim. His need remained, but for some reason he could not quite fathom the patience he had just chosen was enough. Drawing her close to him, he lay back on the bed and asked her in the soft, drawn out whisper of his thoughts to sleep beside him clasped in the warmth of his arms, surrounded by his protective wings and she did not refuse his gentle invitation.

Slumber stole forward on silent feet and before he could even consider how odd it might be that he should not press the issue of his lingering desire, Gairynzvl fell under its tranquil control. Exhausted beyond comprehension, his thoughts grew still and quiet. Left alone in the silence that remained, Ayla tried to settle her own thoughts that were still tormented by doubt and concern. They tumbled over and over in her mind, denying rest. She lay quietly for many long moments, his embrace more soothing than anything else and she listened to the rhythmic beat of his heart and steady breaths. Even as she listened to him, she unintentionally stretched out her senses in an attempt to find Mardan's breath and heartbeat, hoping to console herself enough to finally find sleep.

His condition, however, was in no way similar to Gairynzvl's. In stark contrast, Mardan's breaths were far too quiet, far too irregular, far too insubstantial. In discovering this horrifying fact, Ayla gasped and started up from their embrace with tears already filling her amber eyes. Gairynzvl awoke with unfocused confusion, blinking woozily at her while trying to clear his thoughts of sleep and better ascertain what had caused her distress, but no explanation was required. As he sat up to rub his face wearily, she returned to Mardan's bedside, laid her hand upon his chest timidly, and wept bitter tears.

Chapter Thirteen

The dimness of night transformed into early morning before Gairynzvl finally succeeded in drawing Ayla away from the harrowing emotion at Mardan's bedside so she could rest, which she needed to do desperately. Returning with her to his bed, he leaned against the wall and drew her into his arms, holding her in his warming embrace while he stroked her hair gently and centered his thoughts on restful, positive notions so that her own shifting contemplations could attain some measure of peace. The attendant Healers quietly came and went throughout the hours, repeatedly assuring them in hushed tones that there was no great cause for concern over Mardan's condition, certain that his deep and uninterrupted sleep was restorative in nature. Persuaded by these reassurances as well as Gairynzvl's quiet encouragement, Ayla finally found slumber.

Her dreams, however, would not rest and in the early morning when Veryth returned to speak once again with Gairynzvl, he quietly explained that he could not and would not leave her to battle the dark demons of her fearful mind alone. Explaining that he was capable of filling her sleeping, dreaming mind with more tranquil imagery than her own thoughts and by doing so he could help her attain a better measure of sleep, Gairynzvl inadvertently provided proof of his true nature;. The nature of all Fey of the Light, which was to gently minister and provide hope and light in the face of fear and darkness. Veryth smiled knowingly and nodded, agreeing to return closer to the noontide when they could take a meal together while continuing their unfinished discussion.

Thus, as light and life returned to the Temple around them, Gairynzvl sat quietly in his bed, leaning against the wall and cradled Ayla in his bandaged arms. Whispering to her in the gentle words of his thoughts to soothe her sleeping, he recalled the many times he had done the same thing before they physically met when he had visited her in the darkness. At that time, his visits had been a release, an escape from the relentless torment of the Reviled and her quiet friendship had become more important to him than he could understand. He came to her in silence, afraid she would reject him if she learned what he truly was, but if he had known then how sweet her love would be he would have come to close the portal of the mirror much sooner.

Closing his crimson eyes to the sparkling, streaming sunlight cascading down through the high temple windows, he sang soft verses and lyrical words to her in his mind, filling his musings with gentle images, pale colors, and honest affection that he could not and no longer need to disguise. He touched her resting mind so tenderly that she sighed aloud and the sound filled him with a warmth he had never known. He held her close. He closed his eyes without fear. For the first time in nearly fifteen years, he felt happy. He felt safe.

During the bright morning hours when visitors were permitted, Nayina arrived, carrying a large basket overflowing with baked goods and sweet treats, jams and pastries and late seasonal fruits to bless the Healers and uplift the hearts of her friends. She was greeted by Veryth who thanked her graciously for her generosity. Drawing her aside quietly, he explained that Ayla was resting and apologized that he was hesitant to disturb her as it had taken so very long for her to finally achieve some measure of sleep. He assured her that she could wait in the outer chamber, should she wish to, and she would be notified immediately when she awoke. Yet before Nayina could withdraw, he also took a moment to explain to her about Mardan's tenuous condition, which they were watching closely, as well as Gairynzvl's more promising recovery. He was unaware that Nayina had never met or even heard of Gairynzvl before, but her confusion soon left him with little doubt, although he was just as certain that it was not a tale he had the right to unfold. Excusing himself with a nod, he assured her he would let Ayla know she was waiting as soon as she awoke.

When he had gone, however, Nayina crept quietly into the nursing chamber, peering with monumental curiosity around one of the towering columns at the three occupants resting quietly within. Her inquisitive gaze was drawn instantly to the Dark Fey who slept cradling Ayla in his dragon-winged embrace and she stood watching them for many long moments as her thoughts whirled.

When the noontide approached and the radiant beams of the sun shone down from the temple windows and stretched across the nursing ward to caress the cheeks of the sleeping, Gairynzvl groaned uncomfortably. Ayla was awakened from her restful slumber by his torment and opened her eyes to gaze up at him with immediate concern. Sunlight glimmered across his face and chest causing his pale skin to grow pink and then increasingly more red even as she watched. Alarmed, she moved to get up, but before he released her from his embrace he drew her up and kissed her.

Locked in their tender embrace, neither noticed Veryth or Nayina who stood in the doorway waiting for a more convenient moment to enter in and greet them, but when Ayla finally stood up and tousled her hair absently to shake out sleep, her gaze caught Nayina's and she smiled brightly. Veryth moved unobtrusively away as the two young Fey rushed to each other and hugged fervently. He stepped aside to check on Mardan's condition and spoke quietly with the Healer who was currently tending to him before approaching Gairynzvl, watching with an averted gaze to see how he would interact with Ayla's friend.

Getting up from the bed to escape the steaming sunlight, Gairynzvl tried to move quietly away. He recognized Nayina from the many months he had spent watching Ayla and was certain she would not welcome him pleasantly, but her curious gaze caught his and the introduction could not be avoided. Ayla explained to her friend who he was and Nayina watched him with an openly fearful gaze, in spite of the kindly spoken and friendly words she offered in greeting. Uneasy, he spoke her name quietly and then turned to Ayla, explaining that he could not bear the radiance of the afternoon sun and needed to find a shadowy corner.

His discomfort was palpable and, although Veryth lingered at Mardan's bedside for several moments he did not make Gairynzvl wait long for him to approach. Politely redirecting their attention to Mardan, he explained that his unchanged condition was becoming a greater cause for concern. He was fully aware of Ayla's abilities and inquired if she would delve deeper into Mardan's sleep to discover if it remained as unaltered and deep as it had been or if she could detect any measure of improvement that the healers could not. Although she was hesitant about reaching out to him again in the fear that she would only reaffirm her disquieting thoughts, she was as curious and hopeful as they were to discover possible improvement and did not refuse.

Drawing nearer, she quieted her thoughts, breathed deeply and closed her eyes to focus her awareness. Quietly she moved closer to his bed as the Healer attending him stepped aside, his watchful viridian gaze intent upon her as she reached out to lay her trembling hand on his cheek.

Stillness.

Breathing in deeply, she clamped down the rush of pained emotion that sprang up at this discovery and held fast, refusing to allow her fear to shake her concentration. She wanted to be sure of her reading as much for herself as for the Healers and friends gathered around her inquisitively. It was not easy, however. She had never made a spectacle of her gift before; she had barely even spoken of it, and to be standing in plain sight of all was unnerving. An anxious flutter broke her concentration and she paused to center herself before she tried again, pressing deeper with her questing thoughts.

Quiet. Calm. Drifting.

Shaking her head slowly, she neither looked up nor broke her contact physically or mentally as she questioned further, asking, seeking, and needing reassurance. Inwardly her thoughts shook with emotion, yet outwardly she stood without a single tear falling from her closed eyes. More. She needed more.

Suddenly a vision entered her mind that shook her so powerfully that she gasped aloud, but she did not break free from it. Curious, she watched as the vision took shape and formed itself into a likeness of Mardan, lying, sleeping, drifting. He was cast upon a sea of shimmering light, bathed in liquescent pools of glimmering brightness that scintillated and rippled around him, though he did not move or open his eyes. Was this his essence speaking to her from his unconscious mind? Shaking her head, she refocused her thoughts once again and sought more tangible answers.

Breath? Steady.

Heartbeat? Regular.

Thoughts? No thoughts filtered through to her. Mardan was as quiet and still as he had been before, but his essence lingered and was not as far away as it had been when she first reached out to him. She could not prevent the smile of relief that curved her lips as she gently withdrew and opened her eyes. Her gaze met those who were gathered round, watching her thoughtfully. Nodding slightly, her smile broadened as she confirmed her findings to them, even as she turned and sought an embrace from Gairynzvl who stepped forward from the shadows near the wall and drew her close into his arms. His crimson gaze locked with Nayina's who clearly had anticipated being the first person her friend turned to in such a moment. Uncertain about the expression that crossed her features, he stepped back after only a moment, excused himself and withdrew and he was followed shortly afterward by Veryth who spoke with him quietly as they moved slowly down the long corridor.

"All the things you've been forced to do can either haunt you or guide you." Veryth spoke quietly in an attempt to ease the guilt he carried with him, but Gairynzvl was incapable of comprehending his meaning.

"Guide me? Why would I allow such horrors to guide me? What good would that do?" The sharpness of his tone betrayed his pain, but Veryth's patience never wavered.

"I do not mean you should allow the horror itself to guide you, but because you have such a deep understanding of things many Fey rarely speak of, you have the chance to help those who have suffered because of the acts of the Reviled." Veryth's perspective was bewildering and the Dark One glared at him, unable to see beyond his own pain.

"Why would anyone want my help when I represent what caused them such pain?"

Laying his hand on Gairynzvl's shoulder, the Healer offered the simplest of explanations. "Because you overcame it."

In the Healing Ward, Nayina watched them walking away with curiosity she could barely contain. Turning back to her friend, she smiled and leaned closer. "He is the one who followed you for all those months?" she asked breathlessly as soon as the Dark Fey was no longer within hearing. She was overflowing with curiosity about the Dark One sharing their company and Ayla turned with a smile, moving quietly away from Mardan to a place where the sunlight streamed down into the dimly lighted nursing chamber. There they sat and talked quietly while warming themselves in the radiant rays of light.

"He is, Nayina, and I am so thankful that I did not go to the Elders about him for they would have made meeting him impossible and The Prevailation unthinkable."

"When did he finally come out of the shadows? Were you not terrified of him when he did? How is it that you are not still terrified and why is he here with you now? You seem to be very close to him, but what about Mardan? Oh Ay, I have a thousand questions and you must answer every single one of them!" Laughing for the first time in days, Ayla sat back against the wall, crossed her arms over her raised knees and recounted to her friend as many details as she could recall from the past several day. She described her first encounter with

Gairynzvl face to face, explained how she learned of his astonishing desire to return to the light and how she had come to understand that he would not harm her. She also described their harrowing battle with the Legion of Reviled, which took most of the afternoon.

She also shared her growing confusion and the turmoil of mixed feelings she had for him, including the intimate manner in which they now communicated with each other, through thought and emotion as well as through words. She described Mardan's brutal attack upon Gairynzvl that had shattered her unconditional love for her Celebrant lover and shifted the tide of her emotion. She knew that Mardan was only protecting her; only doing what a Celebrant is trained to do by combating the darkness and the Dark Ones that try to detract from their peaceful existence. As a Celebrant, his indomitable strength and courage had been amazing during their clash with the Centurion, but Gairynzvl's bravery and resilience was no less inspiring and there was just something about him she found irresistible; something she could neither name nor define.

The Prevailation was only a few days away and once it was accomplished everything would be different. Gairynzvl would be free from the tyranny of the Reviled. He would be free to live among them as one of the Fey of the Light, to take his place in their society and find purpose once again. She could not help wondering what changes would occur once the transformation was complete and how she would feel about him. She found herself watching him, considering him, contemplating their relationship and what they could be once the curse of darkness, forced upon him since childhood, was lifted.

There were no answers in their conversation, though it drifted between them until the vespers of evening could be heard riding upon the breeze that drifted through the Temple where the Celebrants prepared for the impending nighttide. Until Veryth and Gairynzvl returned to join them for the evening meal they had little else to do and so they talked endlessly, yet when the male-fey returned they enjoyed a meal together and spoke of trivial things. Nayina watched her friend and the Dark One closely, her glimmering, inquisitive gaze meeting Veryth's often. He smiled perceptively back at her and nodded subtly in agreement with her unspoken assessment that there was far more to the blossoming relationship than met the eye.

Days passed that were filled with quiet conversations and anxious concerns that kept the emotions of the three friends on a blade's edge, but the day of the ceremony finally arrived. Regardless of Mardan's unchanged condition and the fact that Gairynzvl still required a great deal of education to understand the Light and the life of a Fey of the Light, the Elders consent was obtained and the Rite of The Prevailation was scheduled to be performed. There were many reasons for this somewhat hasty decision, but the most impending rationale was the Reviled themselves. As long as Gairynzvl remained tied to their kind he lived in mortal danger and he brought that danger into Hwyndarin through his presence among them.

The ceremony had to be performed upon the rising of the sun on the first day of the week. Because the next morning was, in fact, the first day of the week, it was decided that Gairynzvl and whomever he chose to stand with him would meet Veryth and the Elders in the Chamber of Radiance where the ritual would be undertaken. In preparation, he was fed a lavish evening meal to bolster his strength and was asked to retire for the night as soon afterwards as he could so he would be well rested, but his thoughts tumbled for many hours after he and Ayla shared their sumptuous dinner. He laid down several times only to get up and pace nervously around the room or in front of the hearth, his tormenting thoughts causing his heart to hammer. In spite of Ayla's quiet reassurances and attempts to help him center himself and gain rest, he could find no measure of peace.

Midnight tolled in the Temple hall, announcing and warning against the deepest and darkest hours of the night when the Reviled broke from their lairs and could walk unfettered. The uneasiness of the hour made it even more difficult for Gairynzvl to rest. Alone with his own thoughts at last because Ayla had finally drifted into sleep, he sat down near the fire and let the emotions that had been trapped within him and ignored for years pour out. The torment he had endured at the hands of the Reviled was inescapable. The long constrained effects of torture, loss, desperate longing, isolation and pain forced upon him by creatures of pitiless cruelty shook his entire body with bitter, wracking emotion. Cautious against being seen or heard as a result of the many long years of hiding his weaknesses, he raised a soundless scream to the ceiling as tears slipped silently over his pale cheeks.

Sitting in as much self-inflicted isolation as had been forced upon him by his tormentors, he covered his face with trembling hands and wept in stifled silence until the resonating single toll of the Temple Bell declared the hour. Looking up with a bleary gaze, he drew a deep, shuddering breath and shook his head. He dried his eyes and his cheeks with the only cloth he had available, his sleeve, and realized with amazement that he felt, somehow, vastly relieved and far more at ease than he had felt in a very long time. The chamber was quiet and still, nothing and no one stirred when he stood and crossed to the door. Opening it tentatively, he gazed with newly found admiration at the stately moon delicately poised upon the pinnacle of night and smiling brightly down upon the sleeping forest of his home.

His home.

Though it had for so long not been so, this beautiful, serenely happy place was once again his home. The thought made him smile as brightly and radiantly as the shimmering face of the moon, yet, like falling stars that often caress the night sky, memories of other nights that had been far, far less peaceful darkened his musings. Closing the door, he tried to focus on all the positive things Veryth had told him over the past few days and quietly returned to his bed. Sleep and the sight of Ayla snuggled in the bed next to his enticing him at long last.

* * *

Morning spread radiantly across the emeraldine shadow of the primordial forest of Jyndari with a shimmering glow of incandescent light that poured over the horizon and was greeted by an ever increasing crescendo of birdsong until the entire forest seemed to vibrate. Heavy lingering mists of nighttide, as if shaken loose from the undergrowth by this cacophony of song, lifted through the canopy into the crisp morning air, creating a haze of yellow and pink gleaming light. Within the Temple, matins welcomed the brilliant spectacle of the morn in harmonious tenor, echoing throughout the massive complex of buildings.

The Chamber of Radiance sparkled in the morning shower of scintillating light. Its golden walls and polished marble floor of pearlescent white reflected the bright rays of first light in a tumbling wash of glittering glow. Standing in the midst of this illumination upon a gold mirror set into the stone floor, Gairynzvl waited. Before him stood the Elders, dressed in resplendent robes of silvery-white that reflected the light in shimmering sparkles and mingled with their luminous auras. So bright was the radiance that glimmered around them that they were difficult to gaze upon without tears springing to the eye. Nearby, Ayla watched quietly, her thoughts restricted to her own mind. For her own safety, she had been specifically instructed not to communicate with Gairynzvl in any telepathic or empathic manner during the ceremony.

He stood in this shimmering wash of light, unmoving. At his right side stood an elaborate wheel within a wheel made of gold, clear crystal and inlaid with opals. The ornate object towered above him nearly fifteen feet high and turned slowly upon its shining axis, moved by an unseen force. It reflected the scintillating light streaming into the chamber outward in all directions as it turned. At his left side a pendulum, similar in scale and construction to that of the wheel, swung from its pinnacle. Its precise movement pulsed out the moments as accurately as a timepiece and, although it did not make a sound, the force of its beat could be felt. Above his head a golden mirror reflected the light that shone upward from the mirror beneath his feet and all around the chamber the doorways stood wide, permitting the streaming light of day to flood inward and wash over the participants.

As the sound of the morning matins drifted into silence, the Elders began a rhythmic chanting. Their words were lost in ancient dialects known only to them and their tones were harmonious and discordant together. Opening his eyes for as long as he could manage in the brilliant light surrounding him, Gairynzvl watched as Veryth began to swing an intricately carved, golden censer. Its aromatic incense spilled outward and upwards in fragrant spirals and rivulets and he inhaled the perfume deeply. With a sigh of satisfaction, he closed his eyes once more and listened to the exquisite harmony of voices chanting around him that blended with the celebration of birdsong echoing from the forest. Then Veryth spoke in the High Language of Celebrae.

"Luxaynuth Shybath Henowyn Vacat. Dictamus Trillym Eyrie."

Light Beckons the Vacant Spirit. Speak Your Answer.

Gairynzvl gasped. The time had come. The question that had been asked of him days earlier now required a response. He had agonized over his reply, over how he should properly express what was in his heart and his mind when he said he wished to undergo The Prevailation, but the moment now stood at hand and his answer was essential. The Elders stood listening. Veryth watched him with a supportive, yet curious gaze. Ayla whispered a soft word of encouragement under her breath, which he could just barely hear. Beside him the golden wheels turned on their axis and the pendulum swung in a rhythmic pulse that seemed to mirror the beating of his heart suddenly hammering in his chest.

Why did he want to undergo the Prevailation?

What did it mean to him?

What would he do with the freedom restored to him?

His answer had plagued him ever since Veryth had first asked him to carefully consider how he might answer. Each time he pondered it, the deep torrent of emotion that had been constrained within him for so long surged forth from its hiding place to drown him in its turbulent deluge. Each time, his memories surfaced to haunt and terrorize him, and each time the deep longing to be free from the pain of the past, the loneliness and the dejectedness of being one of the Reviled, consumed him.

He had not asked for what happened to him. He had not chosen to lose his family. He had never desired to live the lascivious, reckless, hate-filled lifestyle of the Dark Ones and each time his thoughts returned to those days he was overwhelmed by grief. Grief for himself. Grief for those against whom he had been forced to commit unspeakable atrocities. Grief for all the childfey stolen from their cradles. Childfey who had in the past, who were at that moment, and who would in the future undergo the same harrowing Integration and suffer the same torments as he had. Even as he considered these things tears rimmed in his crimson eyes and a knot formed in his throat.

"Dictamus Trillym Eyrie!" *Speak Your Answer* Veryth repeated the phrase more forcefully, his insistence causing Gairynzvl to flinch from the unusual vehemence of his tone. Closing his eyes, he drew a deep, shuddering breath, attempting to bolster his courage and subdue his emotion, but before he could contain the flood, the water in his eyes slipped past his defenses to run down his pale cheeks. Before he could clamp a hand over his mouth to silence the desperation crying out from his entire being, the words of his answer tumbled forth in an unabated rush.

"I cannot describe the torments inflicted upon me by the Reviled or the horrors I have been forced to commit upon others. The Integration is a torture meant to destroy the Light within and the longer you hold out against it, the more unspeakably horrifying the process becomes. All I want is to be free from this pain. All I desire is to smile again, to be able to laugh and love and live in the peace and hope of the Light. All I want is to be able to close my eyes and not see criblings being abused and neglected, and more than anything else, I want to spend the rest of my days rescuing as many childfey as I can from the vile clutches of those demons!"

As he spoke, his voice quavered and broke from the force of his emotion. Tears slipped over his pallid cheeks unchecked even as he raised his hands to cover his head in a vain attempt to block the unspeakable images assaulting his mind. His vast wings spread wide and shook as he fought to control the deluge of pain pouring from him, but when he fell silent, not a word was spoken.

Veryth stared at him, having paused from swinging the golden censer as tears formed in his own eyes, and he turned to glance at the Elders curiously. Hooded and robed, they stood silent, yet he could see that two of them had raised trembling hands to their faces, compelled by the honest sincerity of the young Fey's words.

He waited.

At length, one of the Elders moved from their station above him and winged silently towards Gairynzvl, his massive white wings outstretched and beating in a slow, rhythmic motion that spoke volumes of the strength he possessed to move so effortlessly and so silently with such a seemingly insignificant motion of wing. When he reached the young, Dark Fey, he alighted and slowly pushed back his hood so he might gaze directly into his crimson eyes, and, although his stare was nearly unbearable in its remarkable intensity Gairynzvl did not turn away. Returning the Elder's steady gaze, he allowed his emerald stare to pierce into him as if the Elder sought to Know the Truth by gazing into him.

This was exactly what he was doing.

At once, Gairynzvl could hear the Elder's thoughts in his mind. Though he tried to remain detached, the rush of powerful communication both startled and amazed him, leaving him staring back through pools of tears as he listened to the voice of one unlike any he had ever encountered. The Elder never physically spoke nor did he utter words through the connection of his thoughts, but conveyed his queries, his uncertainty, his sympathy, his curiosity, and his requirement to Know if the Dark One standing before him spoke truth or deceit all through the instantaneous transference of his own consciousness and emotion. Gairynzvl could not help but gasp loudly at the onslaught of telepathic contact and he groaned with effort trying to withstanding its potency. The Elder, fully aware of the effect of his mental acuity and satisfied with what he Heard in the core of the Dark One's essence, broke his connection, nodded in a slow, deliberate fashion, raised his hood to cover his head once more, and returned to his place beside his brothers.

The Reviled

Breathless from this experience, Gairynzvl closed his eyes briefly, attempting to refocus his thoughts and his strength. He had been entirely unprepared for such an occurrence, but when he opened his eyes once more he saw the next Elder was already alighting before him and drawing back his own hood. Startled at the soundless approach of one whose wings stretched easily twenty feet from wingtip to wingtip, Gairynzvl jerked backward in surprise. Before he could adequately prepare, the Elder reached out with one hand and placed it directly over his heart.

The sensation Gairynzvl experienced was shocking, literally, as a jolt of intense energy seemed to emanate from the Elder's hand and passed into the very core of his being. Stepping backward slightly in order to regain his balance, he planted his feet in a more steadying stance and stretched out his wings for added stability before raising his gaze to the Elder. Like his brother Elder, he did not speak, and when Gairynzvl sought for his thoughts there was only serene quiet to be heard. He did not need to speak. He learned all he needed to know through his touch, as if he was reaching into the very center of the Reviled One to Feel his essence. While he touched Gairynzvl, the Elder's strength of energy upheld him, but when he carefully withdrew, drawing back his hand as well as his seeking energy slowly so he would not disrupt the normal rhythms of the body, Gairynzvl found himself trembling and oddly dizzy. He was empty in a way he had never felt before.

As the Elder stepped back, covered his head and returned to the others, Gairynzvl had to force himself to remain standing. He reached out blindly to seek support while he gasped for breath and his senses spun in all directions, but no support was offered. The Prevailation was aptly named. It tested the individual on all levels. Staggering, he refocused his thoughts another time and drew a deeper breath, revitalizing himself as much he was able to do in the moment he was given before the third Elder approached.

Hovering over him, the Elder waited until Gairynzvl had recovered before descending to stand with him. Pulling back his hood, he revealed himself to be a young Fey not much older than the one he faced. His white hair gleamed in the brilliant light of the chamber and his wings held a golden iridescence that made Gairynzvl's light sensitive crimson eyes tear and want to close, but it was the Elder's own astonishing eyes that held him fast. They were the fairest shade of cerulean he had ever seen, nearly white like the sky on a winter day, yet within their depths were speckles of cobalt that glittered and sparkled like fine gemstones. His gaze was remarkable and drew Gairynzvl in without a word. The Elder did not touch him, but stood and gazed into his crimson eyes and then past them into his very essence through the window of his soul in order to See him in the bright Light of Truth. He searched for the answers he sought and, nodding with a smile, blinked slowly as if to release the Dark One from the trance-like effect of his gaze before he covered his head and returned to the place where the others waited.

Veryth paused for a brief moment, swinging the censer he held in a slow rhythmic motion while allowing Gairynzvl to regain his senses. He was fully aware of the communion of thought passing between the Elders behind him who shared in that succinct moment the findings of their explorations without speaking a word. His gaze shifted to Ayla who stood apart from them, watching quietly. He was curious to know how she fared in the presence of such intense emotion and energy, and he smiled dimly to her when their eyes met. She had been instructed to remain detached, to protect herself given her extraordinary gifts, and, though his interest in her was fleeting, he felt satisfied that she had followed these instructions and was not in distress. Looking back at Gairynzvl, he meet his crimson gaze with an openly curious expression and asked wordlessly if he was sufficiently prepared to continue. He received a subtle nod from the Dark Fey in response.

"Luxaynuth Reclymanarum!" Veryth's voice rang out, loud and clear, echoing around the Chamber of Radiance in such a manner that made his single voice sound like a chorus. Even more surprisingly, at the speaking of the words to invoke the Reclamation of Light, a bright, clear jet of streaming radiance shot upward from the mirror upon which Gairynzvl stood. At the same moment, the Elders bowed their heads and began a deep, resonant chanting in the High Celebrant tongue. Their words spilled out in an unbroken torrent that seemed to merge with the streaming light filling the chamber. It was as if their tone replicated the reverberant sound the Light would have made if it had its own voice. Stretching out their wings in veneration, the Elders formed a single, unified body whose potent energy could be felt pulsing throughout the entire room. The force of their collective energy in combination with the beaming Light and resounding chant seemed to pummel directly through the Dark One.

Staggering backward with an audible groan of effort, Gairynzvl struggled to retain his footing as the intense Light streamed upward from the floor, around him, through him; its radiance entirely inescapable. The effect of its searing blaze made the burning glare from the mirror seem no more significant than the glow of a candle and, although he grit his teeth against the pain and endeavored to withstand the punishing luster, it overpowered his resistance in mere moments. Tears once again fell from his crimson gaze as the burning sting from the Light scorched his fair skin and blinded his sensitive eyes. It was all he could do to remain standing as he wrapped his wings around himself protectively and raised his shaking hands to cover his face.

"Brynarith Varseenaem!" Veryth spoke the words to Bring Variation, his tone cutting through the resonant din filling the room. His words caused the wheels at Gairynzvl's right hand and the pendulum at his left to double the speed and force at which they moved. The rotating, spiraling wheels began to turn at such a rate that they drew the Light engulfing him into their revolving spheres. Gathering the Light into their center, it seemed to double in intensity, then doubled again, and once again until the gleam of brightness at the center of the gyrating wheels became too bright to look upon. The river of light that twisted up from the golden mirror beneath Gairynzvl's feet and spun into knots at the wheel's center created a vortex that resembled a vast web. It oscillated and scintillated in a rhythmic pulse that matched the swinging motion of the pendulum as well as Veryth's censer.

Gairynzvl had practiced these very commands a hundred times, long before he ever stepped out of the darkness to try to contact Ayla, yet he had had little comprehension of their full meaning or potency until that moment. Standing in the excruciating brilliance surrounding him and listening to the resonant chants of the Elders and the pulsing of the mechanisms at his sides, he was shaken to his core. Unable to see and with his body burning in the intensity of the piercing Light, he could not contain the violent shaking that overtook him any more than he could restrain the growls of pain that escaped his clenched teeth.

Ayla watched from her corner of the chamber, powerless to aid him and unable to bear the sight of his suffering. Her mind spun in horrified desperation, grasping at fragments of thought that floated in the distance between them like droplets of water suspended in the air over a violent maelstrom, but the powerful emotion pummeling through him and from him was far greater than she could abide without reacting to it. All she could do to break away from him was to stare blindly at the ceiling as she fought to remain detached. The sound of the Elders chanting increased in volume as the brilliance of Light also increased, resounding throughout the chamber like thunder as the spinning wheels began emitting a strange, sub-sonic sound. Looking back at the glaring radiance engulfing the Elders, Veryth and Gairynzvl, Ayla watched with inexplicable dread and monumental curiosity, unable to tear her gaze away.

"Luxinaryth Shatyr Piervatra!" Veryth and the Elders spoke together, their voices piercing the noise coming from the wheels. She could hear them as clearly as if they were standing beside her and, although she did not speak Celebrae, she understood them clearly. *Light Shatter and Pervade!*

Upon the instant the words were spoken the fiery radiance congealing in the center of the spiraling wheels burst outward with the force of a bolt of lightning, expanding in all directions simultaneously. It created a deafening crescendo of sound that made her cringe and shriek in astonishment, but before she hid her face from the seeking blaze she saw a ball of plasmatic Light rush over Gairynzvl. His scream pierced the resonance echoing through the chamber as the Light rushed past him, but it was reflected off the swinging pendulum at his side and came hurtling back over him. The whirling wheels at one side and the pendulum at the other contained the energy of the Light, reflecting it, gathering it, and sending it outward once more to rush over him again and again like waves upon the ocean's shore.

Gairynzvl could not stand under the lash of the Light. As the waves of luminance swept over him time and time again, first from one side, then from the other, his strength, balance, and stamina drained from him. The intensity of the Light diminished slightly with each pass, but the intense, searing pain that scathed through him each time the wave washed over him was like a thousand knives being dragged across his body. Each surge was more excruciating than the one before it and each rushing onslaught drew a scream from him more harrowing than the last.

Falling to his hands and knees, he wept more bitterly as the pain became too great to bear. As the Light continued to rush and subside over him, his thoughts began to blur and the edges of his consciousness splintered and feathered into blackness. His cries grew softer as exhaustion overtook him and his mind sought to release him from his torment, yet even in that moment when he would have lapsed into unconsciousness, he heard Veryth and the Elders speak the final command.

"Alteryinaetraas!"

Comprehending this last incantation, he drew a deep, ragged breath and prepared himself for The Alteration. He had thought this ultimate invocation to be more legend than fact, but little doubt remained in his mind as the Light that was sparking and arcing around him reached inward for him. Touching him, it jolted through him with the force of lightning. A blinding blaze enveloped him, drowning out his screams as it spun with a deafening buzzing sound. It twisted and snaked over him, under him, through him as the force of its energy blasted away the remnants of Darkness and any lingering traces of the Reviled.

In one final explosion of radiance, the Light abruptly winked out, as suddenly and with as much brightness as a star falling from the heavens. When the luminous glimmer faded and the Elders ceased their chanting, the wheel and pendulum slowed and stopped. The sound of their pulsating softened and Veryth ceased swinging the censor he held. Only silence remained. The glow from the golden mirror upon which Gairynzvl had stood diminished as well and in the absence of the blinding light it could be seen that the Dark Fey lay there no longer.

Chapter Fourteen

Ayla had closed her eyes and covered her ears to block out the blinding Light and the unbearable sound of Gairynzvl's screams. Her heart hammered in panic and her thoughts railed against the unthinkable cruelty being inflicted upon him. This was not what he had expected! Surely, this was not at all what she had understood The Prevailation to be, but she also knew the Elders were inscrutable. She had long avoided them herself and had done everything in her power to circumvent having to remain as a Temple inhabitant as a result of her gifts. She knew their ways were not the common ways.

What most Feyfolk accepted on a daily basis was insignificant compared to what the Elders comprehended. What most Fey did not understand, the Elders knew as everyday knowledge and what most Fey could not even conceive of as possible, the Elders achieved with little effort. Thus, when silence fell in the chamber and Ayla hesitantly opened her eyes with equal amounts of curiosity and dread the sight that met her amber gaze startled and amazed, but did not truly astonish her.

The Elders remained in their station above the others, heads bowed, wings outstretched, their thoughts centered in portentous silence. Veryth stood on the dais where he had been with the golden censer still in his hand, though now it was perfectly motionless. The wheel and pendulum had ceased their clocklike movements and stood as they had done when the ceremony began. The piercing, throbbing, scathing Light had diminished back to a scintillating glimmer that sparkled and reflected from the golden surfaces of the chamber and shone outward into the bright, new day that had dawned.

Yet the Dark Fey who had stepped out of the shadows only a few days previously was gone. The Dark One who had conveyed his pain to her more intimately than any communication she and Mardan had ever shared, the Reviled One whom she had once feared like no other, the DemonFey born out of the depravity and cruelty of the Realm of Uunglarda was not to be found.

Lying on the golden floor in the sparkling light of the bright day was the one Ayla had never seen, never touched, never spoken to, but had sensed since she had looked up at him through the darkness of her parlor. The one she had fallen in love with before ever having met him. The one she had felt in his quiet moments, heard in the gentle whispers of his thoughts, and experienced in the unforced touch of his hands. His white hair still shimmered in the resplendent glow filling and surrounding the Chamber of Radiance and his clothes remained unaltered, as did the gemstone he wore in a golden choker. Although he lay unmoving, she could see the evidence of his labored breathing and hear his breathless moans, but this was not what drew her gaze and made her gasp in amazement and it was not what caused her to raise trembling hands to cover her gaping mouth in utter disbelief as she watched him.

Pushing himself up from the floor with the force of his will more than the strength that remained within him, Gairynzvl struggled to regain his scattered senses and restore some semblance of normal breath and balance. Lying with his arms extended beneath him and one knee drawn under him for support, he stared down at the gleaming floor and blinked repeatedly in an attempt to refocus his vision before he drew his feet under him and staggered upward. Stretching out his wings for additional balance, he attempted to use the counterbalance of a single wing beat to assist his rising, but even as he did so he heard Ayla's startled gasp and in that moment the steadying command of his wings betrayed him. The sensation of power to which he had grown accustomed was now acutely different. He tried to tip one wing forward and downward in order to use one of the twelve inch spines at the end of each of his wings for support, but only feathers were where these spines had been. He stumbled and nearly fell, but when he regained his balance and straightened, he turned his head to gaze with bewilderment at himself.

He gazed down at his hands in confusion. His skin no longer held the pale, graying pallor of the Reviled! Although still fair in complexion, his skin now resembled that of any others with the most delicate rosy hues and tones of warmth. Stretching out his arms and then his broad wings, he looked backward toward them with even greater perplexed curiosity and discovered not the fearsome dragon-hide membranes and brutal spines he had grown accustomed to as one of the Reviled, but expansive, feathered wings instead!

Gasping audibly, he turned from side to side, stretching out one wing and then the other with equal measures of admiration and incredulity. No longer atrocious and tainted by the poisonous influence of the Dark Fey, his wings had returned to what they had been, or rather, what they would have become had he been permitted to mature in the Light. Broad and powerful, his wings were the rarest colour known to all Fey kind! That which was known as nebulous, the pale white coloration of his feathers was nearly translucent and tipped with beguiling silver hues that obscured, rather than defined, the breadth and length of their splendor.

"Oh Gairynzvl!"

He heard Ayla's surprised exclamation and turned to gaze at her with a similar sentiment choking him, but even as he turned and his eyes met hers, her startled, tearful reaction to his gaze made him turn his head to one side. Unable to keep her place any longer, she stepped forward, hesitantly at first, then, at Veryth's reassuring smile, more eagerly. When she drew to within a few paces of him, she stopped and stared more openly at him as tears and smiles mingled. He reached for her and her amber eyes once more met his.

Blood-red crimson no longer, the hue of his eyes now matched the beautiful shade of his wings. Liquescent and sparkling, the silvery-lavender shade of his stare stole her breath away. Unable to speak or fully comprehend what had occurred, she tentatively reached for his hands, but the overpowering rush of his emotions flooded over her the moment she opened herself to him and she cried out with his sensation of unspeakable joy and liberation.

Ignoring the timid touch of her hands, Gairynzvl stepped forward abruptly and drew her into an embrace that required no words or explanation. Each Fey in the room could feel the elation of his spirit. Each could sense the vast sense of release that rushed through him at being set free from the Reviled at long last and none could speak under the influence of such potent emotion. Even the Elders who rarely spoke or communicated with words, turned to each other and joyfully laughed aloud, but as all stood watched with thankful, gladdened interest, one gaze lingered over them with greater envy than delight. A dark, palpable jealousy broke through the reverie of the moment and it made Ayla raise her tear-filled gaze to seek the source.

As she searched the glimmering chamber, Gairynzvl stepped back from their embrace to gaze down at her intently, raising his hand to steer her attention back to him as he spoke to her quietly. At first, he whispered in the privacy of their thoughts, sharing the pounding of his feelings without speaking before he broke the quietness of the chamber with the sound of his deep voice.

"Only you could see this deep yearning in me, Ayla. Only you understood without requiring explanations, and that is why I am able to stand here now, liberated from my oppression, freed from my exile at long last." He could barely speak the poignant words and they renewed the flow of her tears as she stared up at him in surprise, but before she could formulate a response he continued with a more determined tone. "This is why you must help me, Ayla. You are the only one who can."

Blinking up at him with misunderstanding, she shook her head uncertainly. "Help you, Gairynzvl?"

He nodded purposefully. "Yes. Only you can fulfill this role."

Again she shook her head, glancing beyond him to Veryth who watched and listened without interrupting, though he nodded subtly in agreement. Blinking back her tears, she refocused her attention. "What role? How can I help you further?" she asked more deliberately, curiosity sparking within her even while she still felt the nagging stab of a covetous gaze upon them. Fleetingly she searched the corners of the hall another time while he stood and looked down at her fixedly.

"You must help me help them, the ones who remain under the oppression of the Reviled."

Her amber stare pierced his and she did not need to utter a word in order to convey her doubts, her apprehension or her fear. Shaking her head, she attempted to put her reservations into words, but he continued with determination.

"There are so many, Ayla. So many who live in fear and misery, just as I did; who are not strong enough or old enough to rebel as I did. The childfey suffer unimaginably. If you could see their torment, you would not hesitate." He turned to face the Elders, brazenly directing his words to them as well as to her when he continued passionately. "I know the ways of the Dark Ones. I have lived their heinous existence and am familiar with their schemes. I know their spells, their dark intentions and I remember the hidden ways into the Uunglarda. There is great risk in returning there to liberate others, but how can I turn aside from the suffering I have experienced and witnessed firsthand? How can I not try to free others?"

The Elders did not speak, but Veryth nodded once again in subtle affirmation, though he said nothing. Turning back to Ayla, he posed his question to her once again.

"Will you help me, Ayla? Will you help them?"

Her mouth fell agape as her mind spiraled in a hundred directions, uncertainty, as well as motivation, thrilling through her. Yet, even as she considered her answer, her gaze shifted to a silhouette outlined in the Temple doorway leading into the Chamber of Radiance and the clear, crystalline, cerulean gaze she saw in the shadows.

The End

Dear reader,

We hope you enjoyed reading *The Reviled*. Please take a moment to leave a review, even if it's a short one. Your opinion is important to us.

Discover more books by Cynthia A. Morgan at https://www.nextchapter.pub/authors/cynthia-morgan-fantasy-author

Want to know when one of our books is free or discounted for Kindle? Join the newsletter at http://eepurl.com/bqqB3H

Best regards,

Cynthia A. Morgan and the Next Chapter Team

Story continues in:

Standing in Shadows by Cynthia A. Morgan

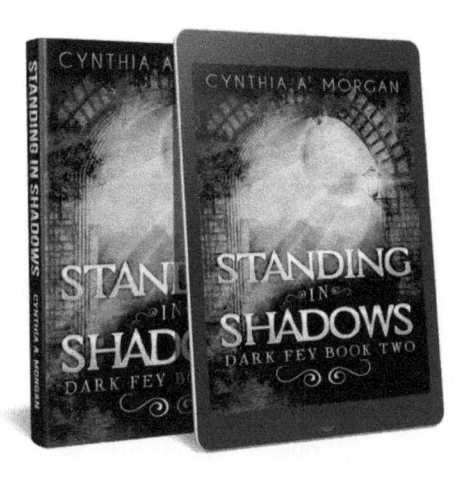

To read the first chapter for free, head to:
https://www.nextchapter.pub/books/standing-in-shadows-fey-fantasy

About the Author

Cynthia A. Morgan is the creator of the mythical realm of Jyndari and author of the epic fantasy "Dark Fey Trilogy", which draws the reader into a mystical realm of primordial forests, magic and the lives of Light-loving and Darkness-revering Feykind. Compared to a fantasy version of a play by Shakespeare, "Dark Fey" is a brutally beautiful story of Love, Hope, and finding Purpose and Peace in the Darkness. It is a tale of Perseverance and Sacrifice with an intense dark fantasy edge.

Morgan is also the author of the popular poetry blog "Booknvolume" where her rapidly increasing following is regularly treated to Morgan's own brand of poetry, English Sonnets, and musings about life. She is a current member of the Poetry Society of America, Independent Author Network, has had poetry published on numerous websites and is rapidly becoming an author to keep your eye on.

Some of her other interests include a deep love of animals and the environment. She is inspired by music and art, as well as fine acting; is frequently heard laughing; finds the mysteries of ancient times, the paranormal and the possibilities of life elsewhere in the cosmos intriguing, and Believes in the power of Love, Hope, Peace and Joy; all of which is reflected in her lyrically elegant writing style.

You can find Morgan through social media in the following places:

Blog: http://www.booknvolume.com/
Website: http://allthingsdarkfey.wix.com/feyandmusings
Facebook: https://www.facebook.com/booknvolume
Twitter: https://twitter.com/DarkFeyMorgan29
Pinterest: https://www.pinterest.com/cynthey728

Contents

Preface — 1

Chapter One — 4

Chapter Two — 12

Chapter Three — 19

Chapter Four — 28

Chapter Five — 37

Chapter Six — 43

Chapter Seven — 50

Chapter Eight — 61

Chapter Nine — 73

Chapter Ten — 83

Chapter Eleven — 95

Chapter Twelve — 106

Chapter Thirteen — 115

Chapter Fourteen 131

About the Author 138

Lightning Source UK Ltd.
Milton Keynes UK
UKHW041837260121
377731UK00008B/445/J

9 781034 274070